Calling Dr. Kildare

Calling Dr. Kildare

By

MAX BRAND

IAN HENRY PUBLICATIONS
1978

First published by
Hodder & Stoughton, Ltd.

This edition, 1978

ISBN 0 86025 135 7

Made and printed in Great Britain by
Galliard (Printers) Ltd, Great Yarmouth, Norfolk
for Ian Henry Publications, Ltd,
38 Parkstone Avenue, Hornchurch, Essex, RM11 3LW

CONTENTS

PRIDE OF OUR FATHERS

The old car of Doctor Stephen Kildare had a flat, high face that had slapped its way through eighty thousand miles of Dartford weather. When it turned on to the Galt driveway it looked as out of place as overalls on Park Avenue. The brakes, ill-set for the last twenty thousand miles, uttered a shuddering groan that stopped the automobile near the front porch.

Doctor Kildare got out not with the stiffness, but with the slowness of seventy years, and reached back inside for his heavy bag. Then he stood straight, for time was adding to his dignity more than it took from his strength. The air of the sharp October night put back his shoulders.

He looked down the hill towards the frosty glitter of Dartford's electric lights and, turning to the house he paused to notice a cypress-shaped maple which, in the brightness from an unshaded window, burned on the lawn like a golden candleflame.

This beauty, set against the soft blackness of night, lightened his step and his heart as he went up to the front door. When it opened, he had prepared his smile for a servant. He had to alter it a little for young Harry Galt who shook his hand hastily.

7

"I'm glad you're here. It seemed rather a long time," said Harry.

"I had to stop at the druggist's," answered the doctor. He looked at Harry's big neck and shoulders, remembering the druggist's suggestion that perhaps the world would be just as well off if old Galt passed on and let his son have his day.

Time is ruthless; our children become our masters, he kept thinking. His mind flashed too, in eagle's flight, to his own son Jimmy—grappling there in New York with some ideal too strong and cruel and beseeching to let him be. Young Doctor Kildare, eh? That made him, the father, *old* Doctor Kildare for sure. His thin lips smiled gently, fondly. . . .

Harry went up the stairs, half turned by his worry towards old Kildare, and the doctor could not help feeling, again, that in the time of need the doctor is the master of the house. He was not a proud man but he knew that even the humblest servants of science are set apart by knowledge from the rank-and-file. Perhaps he was in the rearmost ranks but he marched in the army that stretches the fine spider-webbing of thought across the years of the universe, of splitting away from the face of the atom a portion of its mystery.

"Father isn't doing so well," Harry was saying. "He can't eat—or won't. And the temperature stays there. It won't let up. He doesn't know you're coming; I took it on myself to telephone to you tonight."

"He'll raise the devil, then," said old Kildare calmly.

"I suppose he will and I'm sorry," agreed Harry.

8

"It's all right," answered the doctor. "The devils he raises are not very black and he doesn't half believe in them himself."

"Can you tell me what it really is?" asked Harry.

"Ten years ago," said Doctor Kildare, "you can remember that he had a chronic fever, also?"

"I remember."

"That was a flare-up of an old chronic tuberculous infection," added the doctor. "We beat it then; we'll beat it now."

"Consumption!" said Harry. "And he's ten years older!"

"He's the same old oak. There's no dry rot in him," stated the doctor. "The stock he comes from can be torn down but it takes a big wind to make it fall. Right now he'll outfight half the youngsters in the world."

The stairs no longer creaked underfoot. They were passing along the whispering carpet of the upper hall. They went past the door which Kildare had entered to tend Harry's scarlet fever. They went by the locked door behind which the wife of Galt had spent a year dying. So they came to the door of John Galt.

"Do you mind going in alone?" Harry asked.

The doctor smiled. It rather pleased him to see that the big young man still feared the wrath of his father. He knocked and went in.

"Hey? Yes? Who are you? What do you want? . . . I don't need you, Kildare. Go home and let me sleep," complained John Galt.

"You're not sleeping. You're worrying," said the doctor.

He leaned over the bed and looked through the yellow mist of fever into the mind of the sick man.

Age itself is a disease and other illnesses are only complications. "You're worrying," said Kildare, "and I'm going to stop that. I won't have John Galt softening up, fussing about himself."

"Soften be damned," said Galt. "I'm going to be in the office to-morrow."

"We fought that all out ten years ago. Are we going to fight it out again?"

"If I had a doctor worth his salt, I'd never have got down this low," declared Galt, glowering.

"Maybe not."

"What have you been giving me, anyway, all this time?"

"The usual treatment: nourishing food, milk, ample rest, and Blaud's Pills."

"What for? What for? What kind of pill did you say?"

"Ferrous carbonate to increase your hæmoglobin. And then there was the tonic, I.Q. and C."

"Meaning what? How can I understand that infernal jibber-jabber?"

"Iron, quinine, and strychnine. It's an old friend, that combination."

"There was a time when people didn't have so many fool ideas," said the sick man, "and they seemed to get on pretty well."

"They got on pretty well, John, but they didn't get on so long."

"Can you send me down to my office to-morrow?"

10

"Of course I can."

"Good! Good!" The old man picked himself up on his elbows and grinned at Kildare until the gold of his back teeth was showing. "Now you're talking like a man, and not a confounded doctor. Can you fix me up to go to the office to-morrow, sure enough?"

"I can, and that'll fix you for a longer trip the next day."

"A trip where?" snarled Galt.

"To the cemetery," said the doctor.

Galt let his weight back against the pillows and looked wearily up at the ceiling. "Well, I don't know . . ." he said.

"Neither do I. Neither does any man," declared the doctor. "There still may be in you fifteen years of enough life to give the nervous itch to your men down there in the bank."

Galt's lips parted and his mouth remained open for a moment before the words came out slowly. "You think so, Stephen?"

"Unless you bother yourself to death," said Kildare. "You lie still and keep your eyes closed till I come back."

The banker closed his eyes; his smile was partly relief, partly the weak sagging of his face. In this interval, the doctor surveyed the room like a general swiftly making sure of his battleground.

All the furniture was of dark, heavy wood; the old floorboards were battered and wide; foolish little wisps of lace bordered the windows and all the shades were down. For a moment he was obsessed by a childish fancy, won-

11

dering how the soul, if it slipped from the mortal body, could escape past these walls into eternity.

He had turned to the door when the harsh, dry voice of the banker rattled behind him like dead brush crackling underfoot.

"Why should you be going around comforting other people, Kildare, when you've got trouble enough of your own?"

"Trouble? Trouble?" The doctor was startled.

"I said trouble and trouble I mean. When'd you last hear from that son of yours?"

"I don't know," said the doctor. "I mean—I heard from him today."

"I don't believe it," snapped old Galt. "The whole town knows that he's hardly written home since he went to New York."

"I tell you, I heard from him this very evening," said the doctor. A pulse beat a rapid finger against the hollow of his throat.

"I don't believe it," answered Galt.

"Read that, then, and confound you!" exclaimed Kildare.

He tossed a telegram on the bed. Galt, picking it up, read slowly:

TOO BUSY TO WRITE ALL GOES WELL LOVE
JIMMY.

"Too busy to write?" mocked Galt, dropping the telegram. "And too selfish to stay home and help his father. You've spoiled that boy of yours, Stephen. He'll go to

12

hell in the city. He's not bright enough to keep the pace those city doctors will set for him. He's only a country lad and he'll never be anything else."

"You'll wear yourself out, chattering like a magpie," said Kildare. "Be quiet, now."

"Aye, aye," muttered Galt. "A sick horse or an old dog are better than an ailing man because they can't talk."

His voice died away as old Kildare went out into the hall where Harry Galt remained anxiously on guard.

"It's good that you called me," said Kildare. "I'll stay with him till he's quiet and asleep. Where's the telephone so that I can tell my wife?"

Harry Galt conducted him down the stairs. "It's not serious?"

"At his age and mine everything is serious," answered the doctor, but he softened his words with a smile. "He'll be all right, Harry," he added.

"That *is* good," sighed Harry. "By the way, doctor, how's Jimmy getting on?"

The doctor paused at the landing which was ornamented by a small window of stained glass in which a knight and a lady bent their pre-Raphaelite necks askance to look upon the descending stairs.

"He's already done even more than I hoped," declared the doctor, examining mind and conscience to make sure that he did not exaggerate. "There's no greater medical mind in this country than Leonard Gillespie, the internist —that means diagnostician, Harry—and he's chosen my boy to assist him. For twenty-five years Gillespie has been

13

looking for someone who could be the heir to his knowledge; for twenty-five years he couldn't find his man; and now he has selected Jimmy."

"That's great for Jimmy. Now that he has a hold on a good chance, he'll hang on. There's plenty of bulldog in him."

"Yes," agreed the father, slowly, smiling at certain memories a bit ruefully. "There's plenty of bulldog in Jimmy."

"Which means that perhaps he'll not be spending much time out here in Dartford, and Beatrice . . ."

"Don't bog down," the doctor urged. "Is there something between you and Beatrice?"

"No, but there might be."

"Never stand in the shadow of another man if you can push him out of your way," said old Kildare.

"You mean that all is fair in —"

"Put it another way," the doctor interrupted. "Say that no matter how hard we try we'll rarely get more than we deserve, so the wise fellows keep on trying."

"I only wanted to know," said Harry Galt, eagerly, "just *what* she means to him."

The doctor paused at the bottom of the stairs. At last he answered: "I can't tell you what anything means to Jimmy except that he's fighting now with all his might to gain everything that Gillespie has to give. He's fighting like a football player with his head down. Sometimes I think he might make a little more yardage if he kept his head up. But I don't know. Neither does anyone else. Jimmy's not like the rest of us."

14

"No," agreed Harry Galt, partly comforted and partly in doubt, "he never was like the rest of us."

That was what Beatrice thought too, coming through the dark of the night towards a lighted window in the Kildare cottage. Frost had purified the air, leaving the stars as bright as ghostly day and making the stones slippery underfoot. The face and voice of every life in the village seemed to Beatrice Raymond a weight gathered in her heart; she knew each house, each unpainted lean-to, and she felt that she could identify every door in Dartford by the sound of its slamming.

At the Kildare house she knocked twice and without waiting went into the hall. The ghost of the Kildare supper lingered there. To the left the door opened on what had been the parlour until the Kildares, for the sake of their returning son, turned it into the office which he never had used.

Beyond the doorway she saw Martha Kildare with a lap full of sewing near the desk at which Jimmy never had sat; and on the walls she saw his framed school diplomas, like four steps which he had taken before he leaped into the great world of New York and was gone from her.

"Come in, Beatrice, my dear," said the doctor's wife, looking up with those wrinkling eyes and that large, determined jaw from which Jimmy had taken his character if not his features. "I thought you'd be at the dance."

"Harry couldn't go. Mr. Galt is worse," said Beatrice. "Then I saw the light over here."

"There's always something for my hands to work at,"

15

answered Martha Kildare. "I thought I'd wait up for Stephen and give him some hot coffee when he came home."

"Are you sitting up just for *that*?"

"Well, you know, it's what we do for our men that keeps us loving them. I'm sorry you missed the dance. If Harry doesn't ask you, what about the other boys?"

"They understand about Jimmy," said the girl.

"But Harry *doesn't*? Is that it?"

"He knows. That's why he always acts as though he were a second-hand man."

"You like that young Harry Galt," said Mrs. Kildare, with decision. "I think Jimmy had better come back here and attend to things."

"He won't come back unless he's called."

"And you won't call him?"

"I wish I had a job in a factory," cried Beatrice. "I wish I were so busy all day long that I could fall in bed at night and go to sleep without time for thinking."

"Yes, it's the thinking that makes all the trouble," agreed Martha Kildare. "Has he written to you?"

"No."

"Not a single time?"

"No."

"All these weeks, and not a word!" exclaimed Mrs. Kildare. "He's a selfish boy!"

"No. He's not selfish. He's not forgetting us but he thinks that nothing matters except the great moments. Well, a girl's life isn't made of great moments, is it? We're not always about to die, or something, are we?"

16

"Of course not," said Mrs. Kildare. "But, Beatrice, my dear, how can you know him so well?"

"Because he's hurt me so much," said Beatrice. "And then I have a guilty knowledge, too."

"Guilty?"

Beatrice sat down at Jimmy Kildare's unused desk and put her chin on her fist. "He never really wanted me," she said. "He was just used to me and thought I might be nice to have around; but *I* did the proposing. I'm going to tell him so. I'm going to give him his freedom back. This very night I'll write to him!"

She sprang up and hurried to the door.

"Beatrice!" said Mrs. Kildare.

"Yes?" asked the girl, turning and seeing the old woman through the mist of grief.

"Well, I won't argue," said Mrs. Kildare. "You're too sweet and good to deserve unhappiness; but I couldn't help thinking, just now, how ugly sorrow is in the old, and how lovely it is in the young."

II

THE HOURS ARE RACING

The blue of hæmotoxylin stained the nuclear elements of the cells and showed them as a dark mass; the strong orange of eosin appeared in the fibrous tissue like strands of a heavy spider-webbing that had been wind-tossed into confusion.

It was a slide of lobar pneumonia that Doctor James Kildare was studying under the microscope and this was that early inflammatory stage of engorgement, when the small capillary vessels are dilated with blood and, also, there was free blood in the alveolae, whose cell-lining was destroyed.

The little grape-like clusters which should have been free to hold life-giving air were filled instead, with red and white corpuscles. In this case a whole lobe had been involved. He remembered the particular patient; the suffused face and the feverish, mindless eyes of the dying man looked in upon him for an instant, like something seen through the window of a speeding train.

He picked up the next slide. He had to hurry.

There were twenty more to examine and the night was flowing rapidly away. Every day went too quickly. Each morning he told himself that Gillespie was one step closer to death. Each morning he opened his mind to take in more of those great draughts of wisdom which the old diagnostician offered to him; and every night he felt, as weariness climbed upward from his numb body to his brain, that time had rushed by him like a river, leaving very little in his grasp.

That was why he worked now at five in the morning, staggered by fatigue but still eager. When exhaustion began to eat into the marrow of his mind he told himself that when the year ended with Gillespie's death he himself would lie down to sleep as with the dead.

Whole oceans of blue, chilly oblivion were what he needed. With that promise of rest far off, like a cloudy loom of land from the sea, he set his teeth and freshened his nerve again for the work of the instant.

For him, the whole great building seemed asleep. Save for this one room, the Dupont General Hospital did not exist.

An opening door let into the room a strong current of air that flicked up the leaves of Osler's *Medicine* and set trembling the pages of the latest volume on the heart by Sir Thomas Lewis. Kildare put down a protecting hand and turned with a scowl from the microscope.

The big ambulance-driver, Weyman, was bringing in a huge rye sandwich and a bottle of milk with a glass over the top of it. Regardless of the wind that blew around him into the little office, troubling the leaves of the open books and fluttering a hundred sheafs of notes, Weyman stood in the doorway considering the doctor with a thoughtful eye.

Weyman was large, heavy of bone and thick of shoulder, with small eyes and not much head above them, and a round, solid face running to jaw and jowls. He seemed made to withstand shocks but he had the punch-drunk look of one who has had too many of them.

He grinned askance at Kildare. "Hi, doc," he said. "This is a hell of an idea."

Compunction came upon Kildare slowly, like a tardy conscience to a very busy thief. "I'm sorry, Weyman. I don't want to bother you like this." Kildare rubbed the heel of his wrist across his forehead to get some of the numbness out. He looked at the food and milk. "I'm sorry that you're always troubling about me," he said.

"Yeah?" queried Weyman. "And I'm sorry for *you*, brother. Where's the train you wanta catch? All night, every night. It don't make sense."

He pulled the top from the milk bottle with a jerk, so that it made a brief smacking sound, and poured the glass full.

Kildare looked at the food and drink without interest. His stomach closed up tight at the idea of eating. He lit a cigarette and held out the package to Weyman. "The trouble is that there isn't any time," he explained.

"No time for what?" asked Weyman. His eyes were pondering, gloomy. "You gunna leave the hospital?"

Kildare's staggering brain rallied slowly to the question. "No. No," he answered. "There's no time limit on me. It's Gillespie who has only a few months to . . ."

He saw at the last moment where the sentence had led him and bit off the final word; but his startled eyes were

20

completing his meaning even for Weyman. The driver extended a long right arm, thick with muscle and famous in the history of saloon brawls through the whole breadth and length of Hell's Kitchen. He pointed at Kildare.

"You mean that Gillespie's got his time limit?"

"I didn't mean that," Kildare hastened to say. "Listen to me, Weyman...."

"Aw, quit sweating," said Weyman. "You didn't say nothing and you didn't mean nothing. And anyway, I wouldn't understand, a dumb cluck like me. Only . . . Gillespie, huh? Baby, will that make a change around here!"

Kildare's eyes implored secrecy. Weyman raised the top layer of the sandwich. His fingers were dirty. Vestiges of motor oil and grease smudged the tips and blackened the nails.

"Gwan and eat," said Weyman. "You drive me like a mule packing you in chuck, and then you don't eat it!"

Kildare caught up the sandwich and took a bite.

"And burning yourself up like a screwy light from both ends of the candle—does that make any sense?" demanded Weyman. "Drink some of that milk, you dope!"

Kildare took a quick swallow although his mouth already was full.

"And all because of an old mug that can't teach you anything, anyway. He's out of date. Once he got into the headlines and saved somebody's grandmother, but what the hell? Give yourself a break, can't you? If I was you, I'd slap the old goat down —"

21

Something bumped the door and knocked it open. An old man with white hair blown awry on his head, and a soiled hospital coat buttoned crookedly, sat outside the door in a wheelchair. He moved himself in with one hand and shook the other at Weyman.

"You'd slap the old goat down, would you?"

"Sorry, Doctor Gillespie," said Weyman.

"Sorry be damned. In six weeks I'll be out of this chair and twisting your neck for you," said the great Gillespie.

"Yes, sir; I'm sorry, sir," said Weyman, and fled.

"What does Weyman know? What have you been telling that thug?" said Gillespie, smoothing out the rough of his voice almost to a whisper.

"I don't know," answered Kildare. Then that imp of the perverse, that impulse towards perfect frankness which so often brought him trouble, forced him to say: "Weyman was able to guess from something I said that—you are not very well."

"Ha?" shouted Gillespie, smashing his fist down on the arm of his wheelchair so that the springs creaked. "I suppose you've told him the whole thing, eh? I suppose you've told him that the cancer is eating the life out of me and that I haven't even a whole year left to me?"

"No, sir," said Kildare.

"You've filled his hands full of five-star finals that he can go scattering through the hospital. The whole world is going to know about me, isn't it?"

"No, sir," said Kildare. "It was merely a guess which he won't repeat and —"

"Damn guesses. They're always worse than the facts.

22

You know that or you ought to know it. Look here, Kildare, are you going to be a *mouthy* doctor?"

Kildare stood up and looked into the face of his teacher and prophet. Gillespie, as though he recognised that quietly enduring and stubborn eye, threw down the subject about which he had been roaring and said in an altered voice: "What time is it? Six o'clock?"

"It's only five, sir."

"Staying up here maundering and mauling over books and slides till six in the morning! You don't have to do them all at once. Are you making a damned machine out of yourself! A confounded adding machine with a soul made of numbered parts? . . . What are you doing now?"

"The lobar pneumonia report you asked for, sir," said Kildare.

"Drop it. Do you realise that we have to be men first and doctors second? Answer me!"

"There is a certain knowledge of fact, sir . . ."

"The devil fly away with facts. Facts never beat a drum or blew a whistle."

"Yes, sir."

"Then why do you argue with me?"

"I'm not arguing, sir."

"Don't tell me what you're doing and what you're not doing. I can tell what's in your mind when your eye begins to stick a probe into me. Go to bed and stay there. Don't let me see you till eleven. You're as white as the belly of a frog. You look like something that lives under a log. Why are you standing there? Go to bed!"

Kildare went to the door.

"Wait a minute," said Gillespie, shouting once more. "Don't walk out on me before I've finished what I have to say. The whole world is sick. Do you know what the disease is?"

"No, sir."

"It's sick with youth; youth is what's wrong with it, blundering, blind, stubborn, headlong, crazy youth. Don't stand there gaping. Go to bed!"

Kildare went to bed. In his room the windows were bright with dawn which had not yet soaked into the interior. Even the white enamel of the beds was tarnished. His room-mate's clothes were clotted shadows spilling to the floor. He undressed quietly. It seemed to him that the world never could pass from this melancholy twilight into day again.

Tom Collins called out cheerfully: "What's the matter, Jimmy? Going to waste some more time sleeping? Bad habit, brother. Worse than dope. It'll get you down, if you don't look out."

Kildare didn't answer.

"What's wrong?" asked Collins. "Gillespie been sinking his teeth in you again?"

"Gillespie's okay. And shut up, will you?"

"Gillespie's all right. So's a Kadiak bear or a Bengal tiger but I don't want 'em for chums."

Kildare set the clock for eight-thirty.

The springs of Collins's bed complained as he turned and fell into an instant sleep. Kildare, slipping into the chilly sheets, noted the labouring slowness of his heart-beat and felt the tension relaxing along his nerves. The

24

weight that pressed behind his eyes dissolved more slowly but at last he fell asleep and into his usual dream of weary, hopeless effort.

Then the alarm was clamouring at his ear and he staggered out of his bed to stop its monotonous rattle. Through the open window a cold wind poured over him and the sun of late October washed a pale gold across his feet, a colour, not a warmth. He still was dizzy until he had taken a shower and stimulated his circulation with deep breathing; then his mind cleared as he remembered what lay ahead of him on the trail, the pneumonia slides, the unfinished chapter in Osler, Hazleton's new article in the *Journal*. Hunger to be at his work was greater than his appetite for breakfast. He took two cups of strong black coffee and made for his small office through the crowded outer waiting-room of Gillespie.

Before he opened his own door he looked at that of the diagnostician and read for the hundredth time the legend: *Office hours, 12 a.m. to 12 a.m.*

A cold shadow rose in his soul for it was true that old Gillespie was on call day and night, a tireless machine with a sleepless brain couched in it.

He thought of his master as of a gigantic silhouette which strode across the world with seven-league boots; he thought of himself as a breathless child, vainly running to keep up.

Then he went on to his work. He gave the day a single glance through his window. It was football weather. The mist of the morning had vanished and left a wet world to dazzle in the sunlight.

All over the country millions of youngsters were looking forward with a sort of hungry terror to their Big Games. How many, many ages ago he had been a college boy himself!

Then he was at his desk and lost in work. The familiar ache began in his legs and the small of his back and was forgotten. As he turned from books to microscope and back to books again the wordless prayer that stirred in his throat was always for time, more time. Only a portion of a year remained during which he could enlarge his mind and store it full of the accumulated treasures of Gillespie; and ten years of constant effort would not be enough.

A subconscious voice spoke in him at eleven o'clock. He rose and went into the office of his chief.

III

JAMES AUTOMATON, M.D.

It looked more like an old shoe than ever, battered and shaped by use. It might have been a second-hand shop on the Bowery. Gillespie was exactly right as the owner of the shop, for his white coat was never entirely clean. He had a habit of wiping his hands on it and his violent gesticulations were sure to hunch the shoulders out of shape and wrinkle his sleeves halfway up his arms.

The young Benson boy was there with his mother, who had just unstrapped the heavy apparatus that braced his leg. As it dropped clattering to the floor the doctor was saying: "There we are, Tommy. We've got that infernal nuisance off you now, and one of these days it'll be gone for good and all. You're in a hurry to be well, I guess."

Tommy rubbed his chin. His smile and his eyes wandered from Gillespie to Kildare and back again. "I get a penny a day for wearing that thing," said Tommy at last; "and in a hundred and fifteen more days I'll have the price of—of a pair of roller skates," said Tommy.

Mrs. Benson, with quick tears in her eyes, glanced at Gillespie, but the great man was saying: "And why not . . . one of these days? Why not skates?"

The mother, agape with excitement and hope, stared helplessly.

"We took three steps last week," said Gillespie, "and today we're going to take six. You hear me, Tommy?"

Little Tommy, his eyes fixed upon a distant goal with infinite resolution, nodded, too occupied with hope to hear anything distinctly.

"And let go of that table!" said the loud Gillespie. "Walk right out by yourself."

"Yes, sir," said Tommy, and started bravely towards the centre of the room.

Some of the calf muscles were gone and the foot hitched up, with a twist to the side, so that most of the weight came on Tommy's heel. He made three wobbling steps; he completed the fourth with the fear and joy of accomplishment widening his eyes, and then fell flat.

Kildare, jumping sideward, managed to catch him before his face struck the floor. Tommy's soft body was shuddering with grief and reaction.

Gillespie's snarling, loud voice exclaimed: "Some boys would cry like babies because of a failure like that. But Tommy's not that kind of man, and he keeps on fighting. He's going to do the exercises every day and keep trusting me."

Tommy's sobs stalled somewhere in his throat. When his mother took him out he was smiling over his shoulder at Gillespie with a dim-eyed confidence. The great man defied Kildare with a sidelong glance.

"Well," he said, "he has a chance, hasn't he?"

"Yes. A ghost of one."

"Ghosts make half our life," said Gillespie. "What's any man but a worm that presently will be stepped on, except for the ghosts that follow him and the ghosts that he follows. . . ? I want to talk to you about a couple of cases. Mel Thompson, for one. Remember him?"

"I'm sorry, sir."

"I mean, the fellow who was always talking baseball."

"I don't quite place him," admitted Kildare.

"Good grief, Kildare, don't your patients have any faces for you? Are they all numbers and diseases? I mean that lympho-sarcoma diagnosis. What did you base that on?"

"There were several classic symptoms," said Kildare. "The marked anæmia was there, and the painless enlargement and hardening of the cervical glands."

"Did you wait for the biopsy report?"

"No, sir, I thought the symptoms were definitely —"

"You'd better wait more and think less, then. I want no more snap diagnoses," exclaimed Gillespie. "The biopsy shows Dorothy Reed cells, eosinophiles—a typical pathological report. Besides, if you'd done a little more waiting and a little less thinking for yourself, you might have noticed the Pal-Epstein temperature curve. . . .'

"Hodgkin's disease? Is that what it was?"

"It is," said Gillespie. "Mel Thompson is going to die but not the way you said he would."

"I'm sorry I missed that one," said Kildare, slowly, frowning at the floor.

"Let it go. One error doesn't lose the game for you. But

there's that young girl from Columbia University, the one with the crooked smile."

"I'm trying to place her, sir."

"You can't do it? Is she just another disease lying in another bed with another number? It was only yesterday —influenza, you called it."

"I remember now, sir."

"Give me her symptoms, then."

"She complained of generalised aching pains. She had a high temperature and partial delirium. The chest was clear. I've seen several cases recently and there seems to be a slight epidemic. I was pretty sure that it was influenza. I didn't wait for the laboratory reports."

Gillespie said gloomily: "She has a suggestive facial paralysis and a typical pill rolling tremor, now. She probably had it when you saw her but you stayed only long enough to get an idea, and as soon as one came, you snapped out your diagnosis: influenza. That was good enough for you! Kildare, she has acute encephalitis!"

"Sleeping sickness?" translated Kildare, amazed.

"That's it. I've had to be checking up on you, Jimmy. And that's no good. I have you here to help me, not to be a blasted nuisance. . . . Now suppose you go up to that ward and take a look at Thompson and the Columbia girl —take a good look, Kildare. With your brains and your heart, understand? Then maybe—there's not much chance of it, but maybe, next time you see lympho-sarcoma you'll know it from Hodgkin's disease . . . or mumps."

Kildare, unresentful but sick at his own failure, did as

he was told. When he came back, Gillespie was busy with another patient.

Gillespie called over his shoulder—as he poked a stethoscope into a fat chest: "Stay around, Kildare. Want to talk to you." He turned back to his patient and snapped: "Get on to red meat and salads and leave the starches and the fats and the sweets—get on with you," said Gillespie to the patient.

"Give up everything I like?" whined the fat man.

"You like sleeping, too, don't you?"

"Yes, doctor. I'm one of the best sleepers in the world."

"Then don't change your eating habits," said the doctor. "Because if you stick with them you'll have a long, long sleep, before many months. You'll have such a sound sleep that you'll never wake up."

"My God, doctor . . ." gasped the fat man.

"I'm not your God," said Gillespie. "But if I were, I'd remake you. I'd burn the layers of tallow off you with something hotter than hellfire. There are three inches of yellow blubber lying over your diaphragm; your heart and lungs are clotted with the same filthy stuff; you're rotten from head to foot. Get out!"

The fat man staggered away with the round frightened face of a child.

"Hold the next patient!" shouted Gillespie. "Well, Kildare?"

"You were right, sir."

"Of course I was right. You could have been, too. Do you want to know how? . . . By using my eyes—not for themselves alone—but as lenses for my mind and soul. By seeing sick people—not sickness. By looking at flesh and bone and blood, not charts and stethoscopes and gadgets. In God's name, Kildare—where's the heart of you? *What* is it?"

"My heart, sir?"

"It's only with the heart that we can recognise half the diseases in the world. But you don't know that, you machine, you. You don't even guess the necessity for it. What use are you to me—or to those people out there?"

Kildare felt his face growing cold as though a sudden wind had blown against it. He knew that this was more than the usual tirade. A savage ferocity was in Gillespie's eyes; he was about to strike home.

With an effort Kildare met his glance steadily and waited.

"You were only a boy when I got hold of you," said Gillespie, "but I thought that there was the quick making of a man in you. You had an eye and a sense of things. You looked under the skin. You saw the *heart* of Barbara Chanler, not the condition of her pulse.

"But you turn out to be only a flash in the pan. You've made yourself into a bookworm and a laboratory fiend. I'd as soon take hold of a new case with a steel forceps as with that dried-up brain of yours.

"You treat human beings as though they were exhibits in a morgue. You're trying to learn from me by rote what I learned with time and pain, with the help of God and the power of prayer more than I ever had help from books and microscopes.

"I've little time left to me and I'm damned if I waste it on you. Get out! I'm through with you. I'm through with you for good!"

Kildare got out. Gillespie bellowed: "Send me Cavendish, one of you."

IV

ANY WOMAN AT ALL

Nurse Cavendish came in. She was a large woman who used a corset to give herself a semblance of shape. Deep breathing started her creaking. If she wanted to pick something off the floor she had to get down on one knee.

When she came in Gillespie roared: "Why aren't you ever where I want you?"

"I'm sorry, doctor," said Nurse Cavendish.

She said it like a memorised phrase, her face expressionless.

"No matter where I am, you're sure to be at the other end of the building," said Gillespie.

"Yes, doctor," she answered patiently.

The nurse who assisted Gillespie got out of the office with a frightened face.

"Don't stand there and yes me like an old fool," said Gillespie. His tone changed. "Ah, are we alone, Molly?"

"There's only the two of us, now—and your filthy temper makes three," said Molly. "What's the matter with you, burning yourself up like this, anyway?"

Gillespie closed his eyes and dropped his head against the back of the chair.

"Don't try to coddle me, you half-wit," said Gillespie.

"Who's been fighting you, anyway?" asked Molly, leaning a bit over him. In moments of crisis she had a touch delicate enough to handle wet tissue paper; now she passed her fingers softly over the wild white bush of his hair.

"Take your hand off me!" snapped Gillespie.

"What a baby you are," said Molly. "But who's been fighting you now? Who is there in the hospital with nerve enough to stand up to you since you brought Carew to heel, years ago?"

"I've lost him," said Gillespie, slowly, his eyes closed.

"Superintendent Carew? A good riddance, then."

"Damn Carew. *He's* left me. . . . Kildare."

"I told you so a month ago," said Molly. "I told you that you couldn't flay him alive every minute of the day and night, that if there was any spirit in him he'd fly in your face one day."

"Did you say that?"

"I did."

"You were wrong, then. I *sent* him away."

"You cut your own finger and then cry because it bleeds? Is that the kind you are? You sent him away? A fine boy!"

"A fine boy—but what I have to give can't go to a boy. I have to have a man."

"You worked him like a slave."

"He worked himself; he beat himself with his own whip, the fool! Damn it, I know there's metal in him," said Gillespie. "There's too much of it. He needs softening. That's why I've sent him away."

35

"You can break him but you can't *make* him that way," said Molly.

"The world has more hands than I. It may be able to change him. That's why I've sent him off, though God knows it leaves me with nothing ahead of me except a little time. . . ."

Molly, standing behind his chair, bit her lip and scowled to keep compassion from entering her voice too strongly. "Maybe he'll come back a changed man before long. Or maybe you'll find one twice the man that he is."

"Those with brains to take what I can give haven't the guts to take me along with it. No. I've hunted twenty-five years and now I've thrown away the best I've ever found. Perhaps I'm only an old fool, Molly."

"I've been telling you that for a long time."

He shook his head, smiling faintly. There was no spirit in him to rally to the fight, for the moment. "What changes men, anyway?" he asked.

"Time, women, and hard luck," said Molly.

"Ha!" cried Gillespie. "Time we'll have to do without; I've given him the hard luck; but the woman! the woman! *Cherchez la femme*, Molly."

"Now, what the devil do you mean by that?" asked Molly. "God gave you an American tongue in your head, so why do you talk gibberish with it?"

"A woman," said Gillespie. "I want to find a girl with a brain in her head and a face worth seeing and something in her that a man can trust."

"You've always wanted the world with a fence around it," said Molly.

"In every crowd there are many sinners and one saint," said Gillespie. "Think over the nurses in this hospital. You give them the devil so much that you ought to know them. Send the top three to me. And hand me that telephone. And get out of my sight, will you?"

"Off again, on again, Finnegan," said Nurse Cavendish, and strode from the room.

"Hi, Carew? Carew?" said Gillespie in the telephone. "Where the devil do you keep yourself? I've been trying an hour to get you on the wire. If you've been in your office, it's the fault of the switchboard. Fire them all! Carew, I've kicked out Kildare. . . . It's my own business why; you take him back as a regular intern and assign him to the out-patient service, will you? I'll suggest the nurse for his office later on. . . . Next patient," he shouted, and dropped the telephone to the floor.

The nature of Molly Cavendish was as large as her body and she had long ago taken to mothering the entire hospital—with rod and with rule. Therefore she kept in her mind a sort of invisible card index with listed names, which to her were faces, also. From these she selected three to report to Leonard Gillespie; and three nervous young nurses came to him.

He stood them one by one in the sun that slanted through his window while he looked at their feet and ankles, at their hands, at their throats, at their eyes. Of each of the three he asked three questions:

"Why did you take up nursing? To make a living, to do good, or to find yourself a husband?"

Each of the three gave a different answer. Minnie

O'Hara said: "The only time a man looks up to a woman is when he's tied to his bed." Mabel Parsons said: "I worked in a restaurant, once, so I thought that I could stand the scrubbing and fussing for the sake of better pay." Mary Lamont said: "I thought it was something I could do," and as she spoke she glanced down at her hand as though part of the answer were concealed in the palm of it.

"And what made you think you could do it?" asked Gillespie. There was a silence.

"Why don't you answer?" he shouted suddenly.

Mary Lamont looked at him with a very faint smile. He had not seen a smile like that for half a century of crowded time. Long ago in his boyhood he could remember something like this before ambition closed him away behind the door which he had slammed in the face of the world.

"Because," she said, "I know you'd make all my answers wrong."

"How can I make you wrong if you're right?"

"I think it's been done, doctor, hasn't it?"

"If you can't put your reasons into words, young lady, how can you know them at all?"

She glanced up at the ceiling, hesitated, and then gave him that faint smile again. "Sometimes it seems to me as though words are only a sort of translation," she suggested. She put a question into her statement.

"What colour are your eyes?" asked Gillespie.

"Grey," said Mary Lamont.

"Come here," commanded the great man.

38

She went to him, still smiling a little, considering his face with an interest at least equal to his own.

"Colour blind," said Gillespie.

"Am I?" she asked, politely surprised.

"Yes. They're green. Are you Irish?"

"No, I'm just American. And a little Scotch."

"They're a hard people, the Scotch," said Gillespie. "So run along, now. And thanks for coming in. You're not what I want."

"I'm so sorry."

"You mean you'd like to work for me?"

"Oh, very much, doctor!"

"Why? Don't you know that I raise hell with everybody?"

"Yes, doctor."

"But you'd like to work for me?"

"Yes, doctor."

"Well, maybe you will, one of these days. Now get out."

She got out, but he noticed with some bewilderment that she was still smiling. He rang Nurse Cavendish.

"What did you mean by sending me that green-eyed girl with the foolish smile?" he asked.

"Oh, you're taking Mary Lamont, are you?"

"I didn't say I was taking her!" he roared. "I asked what the devil you meant by . . ."

"I meant just what you mean," said Nurse Cavendish, and rudely hung up her telephone.

"A damned, termagant kind of a woman," said the doctor, and grinned widely. Then he called Carew's office.

"Assign Mary Lamont to Kildare's out-patient office,"

he directed, and dropped the telephone to the floor, where it rolled on its side and came apart.

The light showed on the switchboard where Weyman leaned two elbows on the counter in the midst of conversation.

"Old Gillespie is turning on the heat," said the operator. "He's dropping his telephone all over the place again."

"You know what the old cut-throat has done? He's kicked out my pal. That white guy, Kildare, he's given him the gate!"

"He's been seeing you with him is probably why," she suggested. "Why don't you leave Kildare alone till he's grown up and knows something?"

"Meaning I'm robbing the cradle or what?" demanded Weyman. "Meaning Kildare don't know enough to pick his own pals?"

"Meaning that none of you know what he's all about," said the operator, fluffing her hair and yawning a little.

"Yeah? And who *would* know about him, then?" asked Weyman.

"Why, any *woman* would," said she.

V

SATURDAY'S CHILD

Kildare found that the little dispensary to which he had been assigned stood right behind Sullivan's Saloon, where he drank an occasional beer. When he pulled the door open a customer's bell rang loudly above his head.

The place had been a shoe shop. The old storage room at the rear was now for examinations and private consultations; in the front room were a couple of benches where patients could wait.

He was greeted by the intern he had replaced. "I wondered why they were kicking me out but now I see it was because they wanted to make room for a big shot. But I thought you were tied to Gillespie's bootlaces for life."

Kildare smiled. He could taste the pain right down his throat as he answered: "I couldn't make the grade with Gillespie."

"Your face gave out from him stepping on it?"

"I didn't have brains enough. That's all."

"I don't believe that. But who could please that sour old devil?"

Kildare considered the remark with long-distance eyes.

41

"He's not sour," he said. "He's all right. He's a great man, Sam."

Coster put a hand on his shoulder. "Does it hurt much, Jimmy?"

"Not a bit," answered Kildare, and wondered how he could keep that smile on his face.

"Okay, then." Coster nodded. "Either you can take it or else you're a liar. Come on, Meg; it's time for us common folks to get out of the way. Here's your shop; there are your patients; and yonder is your highlight. Her name is Mary Lamont, Jimmy. She looks to me like a big event."

He went out. Kildare considered Mary Lamont for an instant. He said crisply: "You haven't your cap?"

"I'm still a probationer, doctor," she answered.

"And yet they assigned you to the out-patient service? Well—the first patient, please!"

A woman held out her baby.

"He won't keep nothing down," said the mother. "He's two months old and doing fine till a couple of days ago Dr. Livermore gave him a new formula, and —"

"Add half an ounce of water to each feeding," said Kildare, offering the formula back to her.

"You mean that's *all* I can do for him?"

"And return to Dr. Livermore's last formula as soon as the baby is gaining again. That's all. Next, please."

"He *is* hard and quick!" said the mother to the others on the waiting benches, and they all looked with a scowling displeasure upon Kildare, for how can a quick judgement be as good as a slow one?

42

He was saying an hour later: "How long have your hands been itching?"

"Close on three weeks, doctor."

"How many in your family?"

"There's my wife, and Josie, and Clare, and Pete, and Sonny."

"Take sulphur ointment and rub it over your whole body except the head. Have everybody in your family do the same thing for three nights in a row. Send all your clothes and bedding to the laundry or the dry cleaners."

"But what'll we wear while they're away?"

"I don't know. Overalls, perhaps. But you have scabies."

"I have *what*?"

"Those little dark runs in the webbing of the fingers are the burrows of the female acarus. When your hand is warm in bed at night the acarus starts moving and causes the bad itch. . . ."

"You mean that I've got *bugs* in me? My God, Doc!"

"Next patient!" said Kildare.

She said: "It's something that I catch from my Aunt Millie. She ain't left her bed in three years and every time I go to see her I sneeze for days, and sometimes I get puffy white welts all over me, and . . ."

"What's in Aunt Millie's room?"

"The doctor says that she's got arthritis, but I know that ain't catching and . . ."

"I didn't ask what Aunt Millie had. I asked what was in her room."

43

"Why, there's four walls, if that's what you mean, and a rug, and two chairs, and a horsehair sofa, and a picture of Uncle Ben Loomis. There!"

She finished this in triumphant defiance and looked around for encouragement. She did not like this young doctor; and a rumble of sympathy with that defiance came from the benches. Kildare, his eyes intent on the problem, did not even hear the signs of discontent. He was almost forgetting the loss of his cherished position with Gillespie as he poured himself into his new work; when the halt and the sick came under his hands, fatigue itself disappeared from his strained body.

"You never get the same illness except after visiting Aunt Millie?" he asked.

"Except once I went to the circus; if you can make anything out of that!"

She shrugged her shoulders with a more confident defiance than ever; and the patients who waited on the benches were chuckling in their approval.

"Did you pet the horses when you went to the circus?" asked Kildare.

"What?" she asked, startled. "Now, how did you know that?"

"Nurse, give her a test for horse dander," said Kildare "and make an appointment for a complete test. If you move the horsehair sofa out of your Aunt Millie's room, think you won't have these attacks any more."

"Mother of heaven, what would a horsehair sofa, in it right mind, be having to do with me?" she demanded.

"You have hayfever," said Kildare.

44

"If it's *hay*fever, how is it even the cousin to a horsehair sofa?" she cried.

"The nurse will make you comfortable," said Kildare sharply. "Next patient!"

She was gone from his mind as he turned from her to that double row of curious, the suffering, the dimly expectant faces.

They had altered, now, as his last client disappeared into the back room with the nurse. The expressions of those who still waited had altered from doubt and suspicion and distaste. What they had just heard amused them, but it also struck them as a little miraculous, and people of their class nourish all through life an instinctive belief in miracles. "Thou art a scholar; speak to it, Horatio."

A burly woman had risen, when a big young fellow pulled the door open so that the bell clanged on a sharp, high note of exclamation. He slammed the door behind him and strode on, exclaiming: "Where's the doc here?"

But between his entrance and the slamming of the door, as between two winks of the eyes, a tattered little street urchin of eleven or twelve had slipped into the shop and made himself inconspicuous in a corner.

He looked as bright as a bird, and as bent on finding mischief as a sparrow on finding food. Plainly he expected something worthwhile to come out of the large young man whom he had followed. He had a freckled face and red hair that looked as though a stiff wind was always at work in it.

Kildare said to this new man: "Sit down over there and wait."

"I've got no time to wait. I'm Socker Ryan, and I'm in a hurry."

"I take each man in his turn," said Kildare. "Sit down over there with your socks and all."

The boy in the corner laughed.

"Sit down with my —" repeated the Socker. Then he roared: "What kind of a place is this, anyway, at all?" He stamped his foot so that the very windows shuddered.

"Sit down till your turn, or get out," advised Kildare.

The lad in the corner laughed no longer, seeing Kildare step a little closer to the famous Socker and look him in the eye with a steady and curious inquiry.

"Oh," bellowed the Socker, "it's to throw me out that you're wanting, is it?"

He was about to say more, but a door at the side of the room, which Kildare hardly had noticed before, jerked open and on the threshold appeared Weyman, with red Mike, the bartender of Sullivan's Saloon, just at his shoulder.

"Who's starting the fight?" asked Weyman, hungrily. "Ah, it's you, doc, is it? . . . Back up, Socker. You mug, you, don't you know the doc's my pal?"

"What are you doing here?" demanded Kildare of Weyman.

"Why, this here door opens out of the saloon, is all," said Weyman, grinning. "And I thought I heard the beginnings of a fight."

46

"If you're sick," said Kildare, "come in the proper way; if you're not sick, stay out of this dispensary."

Weyman took the crispness of this command with blinking eyes. At the door of the inner room the nurse was watching.

"I'll handle my patients without help," said Kildare.

"He's right," Weyman agreed. "Back up, Mike. We're sticking our necks out; and he don't need help."

With a sweep of his huge arm he banished Mike into the shadows behind and closed the door promptly. Kildare saw that the people in the dusty room were standing up, agape. He saw the little red-head in the corner, obviously being fed inwardly by the brawl. After what he had been through with Gillespie, and the knife-stroke of that judgement which had cut him off from his Promised Land, mere danger from the hands of any man seemed a trivial matter to Kildare. He could see that the big Socker was at a pause and decided to let him have a moment to collect his wits. So he said to the lad in the corner: "Come here—what's your name—and what is wrong with you?"

"Red's my name," said the boy. "And I've got kind of an ache in my tooth."

"There's no pain in your eyes, Red," said Kildare. "Are you lying to me?"

"Yes, sir," said Red.

"Maybe you'd better run along, then," suggested Kildare. "There's not going to be any show."

"But wasn't there—almost!" said Red, and he laughed.

"What's the rest of your name?"

"I'm the son of The O'Callaghan," said Red, proudly.

47

"Come and tell me about him, some day," said Kildare, seriously.

"Thanks, doc," answered Red. "I'll be drifting along. Good-bye."

He made an exit full of dignity. Kildare, turning, found that Socker Ryan had taken a place at the end of one bench, where he sat with a scowling face. The flush with which he had entered was still burning in his cheeks. Kildare went up to him and leaned over with his hands on his knees to stare into those half-misted eyes.

"How do you feel?" asked Kildare.

"Gwan and take the others. I'll wait," said Socker.

"How do you feel?" insisted Kildare.

"Why, it's a funny thing, but my tongue's numb," said the Socker. "And I don't see too good. And there's some kind of a devil trying to claw his way right out through my skull. I never had a head on me like this."

Kildare took Ryan's blood pressure and found it up around two hundred and fifty. He unwound the soft rubber from that huge arm and put the instrument away thoughtfully. Then he scribbled a note which admitted an emergency case instantly to the hospital and a bed.

He put the note in the hand of Ryan and sat down on his heels to talk to the big man on the bench.

"You're going to take a rest," he said. "You're going over to the hospital and stretch out in a bed."

"What's the matter with me, doc?" asked Socker, fear propping his eyes wide open. "What's gunna happen to me?"

"In one way of putting it, there's too much pressure

48

in you. We're going to quiet you down," answered Kildare.

"Too much pressure—yeah, I always was that way," said Socker, rather proudly. "But why go to bed?"

"There's only one good reason. It's because I tell you to," said Kildare.

The Socker gathered a black scowl which dissipated suddenly.

"Okay," he said. "I'm kinda tired, at that. You do my thinking for me, for a while."

Kildare said to the nurse: "Go with him. Get him straight into a bed. Make him walk slowly. It's emergency. A hypertension case with an impending cerebral accident."

Her colour changed. "A stroke?" she whispered.

"Rub that white out of your cheeks," he commanded sternly. "If you can't prevent your eyes from popping out like that, keep looking down. Talk cheerfully to him all the way. Tell him he'll be all right but that he has to go at everything slowly for a while. Tell Doctor Collins about him. That blood pressure has to be lowered on the run or he'll crack. Then come back here."

From the door, a moment later, the Socker said: "Hey, doc, will I be seeing you? What I mean, I hate strangers."

"I'm only on part-time duty here and I'll watch you in the hospital," said Kildare, and he watched the girl walk off at the side of Ryan, smiling, chatting brightly, but always with her eyes lowered.

"Yeah," said a fat old man on one of the benches, "they oughtn't to use a gal like that for a nurse. How's she gunna keep her mind on her work when she's got a face like that for a ticket around the world?"

And a woman added: "You take the beauties like her, they don't use the brain none. They just lean on their faces, you might say."

But Kildare did not listen; he was calling aloud: "Next patient, please!"

VI

WORKER OF MIRACLES

The afternoon darkened as it grew older and then a misting rain brought on a premature twilight. Kildare was very tired but it was better to have his hands filled with work than to return to the hospital and sit among the ruin of his hopes. Also, there was the letter he must write home to tell them that the great Gillespie experiment had failed wretchedly and that he was back in the herd. That was why he was giving himself with such an impatient eagerness to each case; and then out of the misting twilight an uproar arose through the street and through the saloon.

The side door flung open and showed a policeman with a senseless child in his arms. Her head and feet flopped in time with his running feet. Her hair hung down in blonde, ratty strings, like a kitchen mop that needs a good washing. Kildare caught the youngster up and laid her on the examination table.

She was very cyanotic. It was strange that living flesh could be so blue. With his head over her heart, he found the beat of it, small, rapid, thready. Now and then the chest heaved upwards in a spasmodic effort but without accomplishing respiration. For whatever was to be done, there were only quickly passing seconds.

Kildare looked up from the small body, his face greasy with cold sweat, and saw two other interns from the hospital in the room. They naturally had come along from the saloon, where they had been drinking beer when the policeman came through with the child. The mother of the girl half crouched by the table. She kept putting out her hands with a cherishing gesture towards the child and her eyes shifted down and up, always rising with a dumb appeal to Kildare.

Through the strain and crisis of the moment a door was opened somewhere in his brain and the picture of the woman was printed for him for ever with chin and lips and nose pinched outward into blunt points and the pull of a thousand lines narrowing her eyes at the corners. She had four wrinkles like four sharp incisions across the front of her throat. Yet ten years before she must have been a beauty.

Tomasson, one of the interns, said: "It's a concussion, Jimmy . . . and there's no time . . ."

Kildare's hand, over the youngster's heart, felt the pulsation stagger and then halt like an overburdened horse dragging a weight up a hill. From the relaxing fingers of the girl, as death came over her, something dropped.

It bounced with a sharp, metallic rattle and Kildare saw a little iron jack jog to a stand on the floor. The mother saw it, also. Out of her throat came a wordless cry with nothing human except the grief in it. She caught her girl by the heels and jounced her violently up and down in the air. A second jack fell from the unconscious lips and clattered on the floor.

There had been a general cry of protest at this apparently insane brutality of the mother, but now she surrendered the child to the doctor again quickly. Only her eyes were desperate with appeal that science should continue the work which she had begun. And Kildare remembered what Gillespie had said about being a man first and a doctor second.

Life itself was perhaps the primary teacher or how else had this woman of the slums known what to do for her own? He was trying vainly, now, to find the beat of the heart. There was no noise to confuse him for everyone in the room, with held breath, was watching the face of the child.

Her blue lips had parted and her eyes opened a trifle. In that moment of utter concentration he saw the nurse, Mary Lamont, white and still, as one sees something in a book.

The heart of the child was not beating. There was not a tremor of life. She was dead.

He looked up and straight at the mother; every soul in the room helped her draw breath. She had understood that silent glance of his, but instead of the scream which he expected, she was waiting in this last hope.

One chance remained. He called for adrenalin, reached for a syringe, and tore the dress of the girl open at the breast. High on the chest he located the Angle of Louis which marks the second interspace between the ribs and counted down to the fourth interspace, over the heart. Nurse Lamont had the syringe ready for him as he swabbed the skin. Laterally from the internal mammary artery he had to make the injection. He selected the exact spot and drove the needle right in towards the heart.

Somebody uttered a groan with a shudder in it. That was the mother. Someone was holding her hands. It must have been Weyman, for his large voice began to say: "Take it easy—this doc raises 'em from the dead—this doc don't miss. . . ."

Kildare inserted the needle swiftly and deeply. When he pulled out on the syringe top a little, blood followed and he knew he was inside the heart. Now that he was sure, he injected a whole cc. of adrenalin straight into the chamber of the heart, pulled out the deeply bedded needle, and swabbed off the punctured skin with alcohol. He began the movements of artificial respiration.

The mother had stopped struggling in the hands of Weyman; but Kildare could not look at her because he knew what he would find in her eyes. He felt a stir of the body and instantly removed his hands from it.

Immediately came a convulsive lifting of the breast. It was not a vain labour this time. Everyone in the room could hear the swift intake of the breath. Yet the tiptoe, incredulous quiet still continued.

Then Weyman in a rumbling murmur said: "He's done it again; he always does it; he brings 'em back!" That voice loosed a whole tide of uproar and delighted congratulation. These people were sweating as though they had done the work.

Afterwards, when the child was removed to the hospital, Kildare looked about him and discovered with amazement that not a client remained for him on the two benches.

"Weren't half a dozen people waiting for me there?" he asked the nurse.

"They all felt healthy after they saw the blue face of poor little Jenny Carson," she answered.

Kildare said dreamily: "We had some luck, there, after the mother showed us the way. Did you watch her face—the mother's?"

"I watched her when she was thanking you, doctor."

"Did she thank me?" muttered Kildare, and rubbed the heel of his wrist across his forehead.

"Now that there's no one here, if you'd lie down on the examination table for half an hour . . ." said the nurse.

"Certainly not!" said Kildare, and looked curiously at her. She stiffened and banished all expression from her face.

He would have said something to soften his last words but here the door of the dispensary opened and Red, son of The O'Callaghan, stepped inside.

"Hi, doc. Can I say something to you?"

"Fire away," said Kildare.

"Kind of private, I mean," suggested Red. With a jerk of his thumb Red indicated secret distances. Mary Lamont retired to a corner.

"Look," said Red, from the side of his mouth. "There's somebody all in a heap. Will you grab some tools and come along?"

"I'll call an ambulance," said Kildare.

"No. Don't you," advised Red. "It's on the jump that we gotta make it. I'll try somebody else."

Kildare did not hesitate. He caught up his topcoat and

an emergency bag and went out into the soupy half-light of the rain and the evening. Red made his strides long to keep pace. Once in a while he took a hitch-step to cover lost ground. "It ain't far," pouted Red. Kildare made no answer. A traffic light stopped them.

"This Jenny Carson that you fixed up," said Red, "I hear you stabbed her right through the heart and that was what woke her up."

"Not exactly through the heart," answered Kildare.

"It wouldn't have done any harm. It would take something like that to wake her up," said Red. "The trouble with girls is they're always kind of sleepy. The trouble with Jenny," said Red, "was she was always swallering things and sleeping them off and swallering again."

Red led the way around the next corner and presently stopped to take a look up and down the street. A few shadowy figures moved in the gloom but nothing really lived except the wavering yellow moonpaths which the street lamps laid out on the pavement.

"We duck in here," said Red, and hurried in from the street under the porch of an old house, whose glimmering black windows contained "For Rent" signs.

"The guy we're gonna check with, he's kind of nervous," said Red. "So I'll go first."

"How was he hurt?" asked Kildare, as Red opened the cellar door upon utter darkness.

"Just sort of stumbled and cut himself," said Red.

"I think you're lying, Red," declared Kildare. "This smells like the sort of thing the police should know about."

"This? Police?" asked Red in a voice of astonishment.

56

"What d'you think? I'd get a good guy like you into trouble? Look, doc, this is a right guy I'm taking you to, but he's terribly nervous just now."

He lighted a match and from the bowl of his fingers cast a ray into the blackness. He guided Kildare down a flight of steps into subterranean cold. A cobweb touched Kildare's face with tenuous, sticky fingers, and left dust in his nostrils. At the bottom of the steps the match went out.

They stood in darkness, breathing the cold, stale air. Above them, dim footfalls went hurrying along the sidewalk out of nothingness into nothingness. "The lantern's over here," said Red, whispering.

VII

THE IRISH WILL FIGHT

There followed the grating of rusty metal on metal, the scratch of another match, and then a circle of smoky light as the flame ran across the wick. When the chimney was lowered, the light enlarged their world to concrete walls on either side. They were stained like old mattresses.

The boy stood up and looked about him. That underground environment and the breath of danger in it sharpened his eyes and set in them an Irish gleam of happiness. He beckoned to Kildare as he led on to a door which stood slightly ajar, lodged against the floor by a broken upper hinge.

"Hi, Nick!" called Red.

"Red?" answered a voice.

"He's okay; he ain't fallen apart, yet," observed Red. "Come on, doc."

Red dragged the door open and advanced, holding the lantern high. All about them old furniture loomed in piles with tatters of ruined upholstery hanging down, and through a narrow aisle in the centre of this confusion the lantern light streamed faintly across a man who was crouched on a mattress against the wall. All the light seemed to gather to the automatic which he levelled across his raised knee.

"Who's that?" called his excited voice. "Who you got there, Red?"

"I brought a doc for you, Nick," answered Red.

"You fool," groaned Nick. "What you trying to do to me?"

"Quit it, fella, will you?" pleaded Red. "This one ain't like the others. Old Wildman Weyman—this is his pal! He's gunna fix you up. It's Doc Kildare."

Nick got off the mattress to one knee. His left hand clutched his breast. Agony kept his eyes big and a grin on the white of his face, but his gun-hand was steady. In the lantern-shine the metal was silver-bright, without a tremor.

He was very young. He was not more than seventeen or eighteen. At that age, Kildare remembered, they do their killing first and their thinking afterwards. Blood kept oozing through the spread fingers of the boy's hand. It ran down to his elbow and fell off in audible drops on a newspaper.

"Keep clear of me," said Nick, "or I'm going to blow you down."

"We'll see about that," answered Kildare and moved straight ahead.

They were the hardest steps he had ever made in his life but he could not hold back after the curious glint he had seen in the eyes of Red. The small boy became the consciousness of the whole world watching him go over the top.

As he strode past the lantern, his own shadow poured darkness before him over Nick and across the wall. The mouth of the gun, tipping back to look him in the eye, was as big as the round, black throat of a cannon. Nick's mouth twisted to one side and showed his teeth. Then Red's voice exploded: "Nick! Put that gun down, you damn fool!"

The lantern came swinging past Kildare as Red tried to break in between him and trouble. He stopped the boy and took the lantern away from him.

"You run to the hospital and get an ambulance," he commanded.

"Okay," said Red, vanishing through the door.

"Leave the ambulance out!" shouted Nick.

"Okay; Okay!" called Red from the distance, where he could be heard running through the outer blackness of the cellar as sure of foot as though he had the eyes of a cat.

"Now put that gun down," said Kildare, leaning over Nick.

Nick said: "Keep away or I'll . . ."

Kildare pushed him back on the mattress and all the strength of resistance went out of him, suddenly. He lay without word or motion as Kildare opened the coat and the sticky wetness of the shirt.

The lad was all tendon and bone, with little flesh. His ribs stood out like big fingers without knuckles; his belly fell away flat. He had the orchid-white skin of a city dweller. Kildare had the sick feeling that there was no force left in the boy to fight for his life. And much of it

60

had run away already. There was blood over everything, splotches and tricklings and little pools that shone in the lantern light.

Nick kept his head raised to look down at the wound in his breast. Kildare put his hand under the chin and pushed the head back against the mattress.

"Lie still," he said. "Breathe easily. Let go of everything. We're going to pull you through."

"Are you?" said Nick. He even laughed a little, forcing a large out-welling of blood from the wound in the breast.

"Stop that laughing. Breathe in your belly," said Kildare. "Breathe right down here, slowly."

"Turn up the lantern," said Nick. "Turn the wick up, will you? It's going out, and it would be hell to be caught in the dark, wouldn't it?"

Kildare turned and stared at the lantern which was flaring up so high that one end of the wick threw out a little wisp of smoke that was staining a side of the chimney yellow-brown.

He grabbed his emergency bag for fast work. He laid out the shining instruments rapidly. When the eyes darken it is not far from the end.

"You've got more stuff to handle than a plumber," said the boy, and grinned all on one side of his mouth. He had a handsome face, nobly made about the forehead. Nick said: "But you might as well stop trying, doc. I'm late for school again."

"What do you mean?" asked Kildare.

61

"It's not the lantern; *I'm* the one that's going out," said Nick.

"Close your eyes and stop watching the light," said Kildare. "You're dizzy; you're not dying."

"I'm anything you say; but don't get your hands dirty for nothing," advised Nick.

It would have been magnanimous in an old philosopher; it was very strange coming from a lad of the slums. For Kildare the boy for the first time was something more than a casual accident case.

There were two possibilities. Under the broad, raw slash of the wound, the bullet might have penetrated only through the rib, or it might be penetrating the heart itself. Kildare prayed for the ambulance; in the meantime he worked as though he had not the slightest hope of its arrival.

He had to have sterile instruments for this work, first of all. He found a packing-case from which kitchen utensils protruded through a broken side. He got a saucepan out of the confusion, crushed some of the loose boards into kindling under his foot for a fire, and from a tap in the cellar hall he drew water. In a moment he had the pan over the flame, with the instruments in it.

Nick bent his head to one side. "Ever done any camping out, doc?" he asked.

"Yes," said Kildare. "Have you?"

"This is my first time," said Nick. "There's a good kind of smell to woodsmoke . . . but what about it getting outside and starting a fire-alarm?"

Kildare had lighted the fire just outside the door of the

room to keep from choking his patient with the fumes. He looked up and saw the white mist crawling down the ceiling. There was something more important to him than interference from the outside. The boy was in shock and had to be kept warm. So he fed some more splintered kindling into the fire and then went rummaging through the furniture until he found a chest of bedding. With quilts and blankets he wrapped Nick thoroughly from head to foot.

"Jeez!" said Nick. "All done up—like a sugar Easter egg!"

Though there was no mirth in his dim eyes, he kept starting to laugh, and Kildare with a raised hand and a scowl warned him, from that involuntary spasm.

Then footfalls hurried down the cellar steps. He saw Red coming with an electric flashlight and another figure moved behind the boy.

"Ambulance?" called Kildare.

"I got something better—for Nick," said Red, hurrying on.

The shadow behind him was turning into a girl with bright hair and a pretty face.

"It's Rosalie, is all. She's Nick's sister," said Red. "Listen, doc," he added in a murmur, "you couldn't get Nick to a hospital. He'd die, first. He's in there, Rosalie," he added to the girl.

She went by Kildare towards the door. She had only a half second to get the white tension out of her face and smile at him, but she made the best of the opportunity. He felt, vaguely, that a light had shone in his eyes, but then he saw that the water had begun to boil in the pan and that took all his attention.

"Watch this water," he said to Red. "Don't let the pan joggle and spill . . ."

Nick was saying, huskily, feebly: "Get out of this, Rosalie. I never wanted anything from you after I found out about you. I don't want anything now. Don't stay here and take any rap account of me."

The words were sounds without much meaning, to Kildare. He went into the room to find her with an arm under her brother's head, speaking softly, and he with a hand raised as though to ward her off but submitting little by little to the caress of her voice and her touch. Kildare bared the breast of the boy and painted it liberally with iodine.

"Send her away, doc, will you?" begged Nick. "I don't want to get her in the soup."

"I have to talk with you," said Kildare, and took her out into the corridor.

There was only the light from the fire wavering over her and dancing her shadow on the wall. Red, overseeing the cooking of the instruments, glanced curiously up at them.

"Are you steady? Are you all right?" asked Kildare.

"Yes, doctor," she said. She had a docility like that of a trained nurse, but strangely different. Her eyes kept following, anxiously, every glance of his; they seemed to struggle to get inside his brain at hidden meanings.

He told her about Nick, making a distinct effort to reduce her from a personality into a charted number, a mere entity requiring professional consideration before he went ahead with the case.

"This case ought probably to be taken to the hospital before anything is done," he said. "Nick doesn't want the hospital. Do you agree that he should not be taken?"

"Yes, doctor. Oh, yes!" she said.

"Are his parents available for consultation?" he asked.

"No, doctor. He only has me—poor Nick!"

In spite of his effort to be perfectly impersonal, he could not help feeling that this girl was a creature made for smiling, not for serious thought. Even at this moment when she was white with fear for her brother, a smile kept beginning and dissolving and beginning again in her eyes as though it were her nature to propitiate everyone. Kildare felt pity and something beyond pity that disturbed him; he assumed a frown to banish this unmedical emotion.

"I have to probe the wound and I want you to watch if you can stand it," said Kildare.

"Yes, doctor."

"Are you sure?" he asked, doubtfully.

"Oh, yes."

"Well, it's this way. If the probe hits the bullet, it may pulse in and out with the throbbing of the heart. That would mean that the bullet actually is in the heart muscle . . ."

"But then he would be dead!"

". . . and in that case I must absolutely insist that the case be taken to the hospital with or without the wish of your brother and yourself."

"Ah, but why? Why would you do that? Everyone knows what miracles you can work by yourself. Please, Doctor Kildare, if you'll only . . ."

"Because in the hospital," he interrupted, "it would be easy to give a transfusion to maintain his strength before the shock of the operation. I might have to split the sternum—the bone in here—to give adequate exposure of the object to be removed. . . . This is a tough job to do alone; assistance would be worth a lot."

"Let *me* help. Please let me help!" she begged.

Actually she was smiling for him, as though she knew how much harder it is for a man to refuse a request from a pretty face.

"The assistance of intelligent hands is what I refer to," said Kildare, sharply, and went back into Nick's room.

"How are you?" he asked, crouching beside the mattress.

"Dizzy," said Nick. "Dizzy with luck, doc, because I've got you here."

Even the stiff lips of Kildare relaxed a little towards a smile as he heard the inevitable Irish blarney.

"A sweet, difficult, damned lot you Irish are," he said.

"Ah, doctor," murmured the girl, "but aren't you just a little Irish yourself?"

"Perhaps," said Kildare, darkening his forehead again, and began to probe the wound. He felt, presently, the small click of the probe against metal and took his hand away, letting the probe remain aslant in the flesh. He heard the girl take a breath and saw her turn a hand into

66

a fist; he would not permit himself to look up towards the fear and shock in her face. With his hand on Nick's breast he was following the fluttering, rapid beat of the heart, a shudder rather than a true pulsation. He removed the probe.

"Come with me," he said to the girl, and went back by the fire in the outer corridor. Behind him he heard the girl saying something with a "darling" in it to her brother, and Nick's husky voice muttering: "Get out—get out of this and stay out! I don't want you . . ."

Then the girl was there before him. She moved so that she could be directly in front of him, as he spoke.

He said: "I can't be sure. There's a chance both ways. His heart action is very faint and confused. The slight pulsation of the probe may mean that it is in the wall of the chest near the heart, or it may actually be in the heart muscle itself. I don't know what to do."

He waited for her to implore him to perform the operation on the spot. Instead, she merely said: "No, doctor."

"On the other hand," he argued softly with himself, "if the bullet actually is in the heart the joggling in the ambulance . . . Very well," he said aloud, and turned to his work.

He got rubber gloves out of their antiseptic canvas container, gave the morphine injection to keep Nick quiet, and novacaine to deaden the pain. After that he went to work with the razor edge of the scalpel, clamping off the bleeders as he went. He could not tell the exact depth of the lodgement of the bullet, for the rib being shattered the bracing of that bone was removed and the normal indications were blurred.

The girl was always there, together with Red.

Once he heard Nick murmur: "Look at you, Rosalie. You can't take it. You're only a baby. You're a softy. Red can take it, but you can't."

"Shut up and save it, Nick," advised Red.

The hands of these two were not clasped together, but somehow Kildare knew that their attitude was that of the devoutest prayer. He was down to the lead of the bullet, now. Presently he looked up, not at their tense faces but at that invisible God who attends our greater moments.

"It's all right. The heart's all right," said Kildare.

"Ah, Nick," whispered the girl. "Ah, Nick, darling . . ."

"Look at her," said Nick to Red, speaking through his teeth but inevitably maintaining the spirit of badinage. "She's only a stuff. She'll be bawling all over the lot, in a second or two . . ."

His voice trailed off.

With the forceps Kildare lifted the bullet out, flicked the blood from it, and dropped it into his bag. With the same forceps he picked out little spicules of bone from a shattered rib. He had tied off some bleeders, going down. Now he had to sew in two layers, first the fibrous tissue around the rib, then with deep skin sutures. He put in a small rubber drain and reminded himself that there should be a tetanus injection for all gunshot wounds. That would have to be later.

Nick did not faint. His pulse had held up and with the pressure of the bullet removed it improved suddenly. He was still in shock. His forehead was cold as a wet stone and his eyes were dim but with an Irish glitter in them, like the old devil looking through a fog. . . .

VIII

TWO WOMEN

Kildare rose to stretch the ache out of his back. A dusty mirror against the wall repeated the gesture behind a mist.

Rosalie said, "Everybody's saying that you could do anything you want to. They're all talking about you from the docks to Sixth Avenue. They're all saying there was never anybody like you. But if they could know about you taking a bullet right out of a heart—what would they say then?"

"It was *not* in the heart," said Kildare hastily.

"Couldn't I see with my own eyes?" she asked, making them large. Her voice made echoes inside him, running tiptoe up his spinal column to the brain.

"Don't talk nonsense," he said weakly.

He stood up and dusted his hands. The girl rose too, trying to bring the line of his eyes to her face. But he only would permit himself to see her hands.

"Will you come with me?" he asked, and led her out of the room. Behind him, Red was saying softly, furiously: "You didn't say a word. You didn't thank him, Nick!"

He even could hear Nick answer: "You don't thank a guy like that. You wait till there's a chance to *do* something."

70

Kildare led her into the next room, empty, damp, with the curious smell of old cement. He said: "My hospital will have to have a report on this."

She shrank from his words. "But that means that the police will know!"

"The police are not to know, eh?" asked Kildare.

She was silent, her eyes begging without words. Kildare looked down at the floor to avoid her face and that was why he did not see her expression change swiftly into one of the keenest inquiry. A gambler with a heavy stake on the board might have watched the spin of a roulette wheel as she watched Kildare now.

He said: "A doctor who doesn't report a gunshot wound goes to gaol. It's the end of his life—as a doctor." He waited to hear her appeal but she said nothing. Gradually he lifted his head.

"That report has to go in," he said grimly. "Who shot your brother?"

"I did," said Rosalie.

The shock made him look her straight in the eyes and he was aware at the same moment of the perfume she was wearing. It was not rose or violet or any flower for which he had a name.

"*You* shot him?" repeated Kildare. "Suppose you tell me how you happened to do it?"

"I don't know. It's all crazy in my mind," said the girl. "We had a row. And I went wild. There was a gun. And it went off."

"So you let him stagger out with a bullet in him?"

"I didn't know . . ."

71

"What do you gain by not telling the truth?"

"I only wanted you to listen. Because I *must* talk to you! *Will* you listen?"

"Yes," said Kildare.

Listening was watching, too. He was not peering through a microscope but he still could see things which were of greater significance than all he had found in stained slides on dark fields or bright. It was extraordinary to observe how she still smiled to win grace even when there were tears and sorrow in her eyes. It seemed to him that as she held out her hands to him she was asking him into her life, and her glance was on his face with an almost physical touch.

He felt strangely at ease, as though he had known her for a long time. It seemed to him that this great friendliness in her was like that of a child which knows and fears no harm in the world.

She was saying: "He's not bad, is he?"

"He can't be very bad," agreed Kildare.

"And there's no lying in him. He's so proud that he'd give the heart out of him rather than sneak and lie."

He looked for one instant away from her, remembering the fierce, steadfast eyes of the boy. "That's true, I think," he told her.

"But I haven't made a home for him to keep him off the streets after he and I were left alone."

"How could you keep yourself and make a home for him at the same time?" asked Kildare.

"Some way I should have done it," she said. "But you

wouldn't know how poor we've been!" She held up a hand to call the ceiling to witness how great their poverty had been. Her neck-piece of the finest black fox slipped back over her shoulders.

When she saw that he was moved, she was able to weep big tears. Yet as she wept she kept smiling. Even grief was beautiful in her, he saw. Oh, she was clever, that Rosalie girl.

"Will you please listen to me, doctor?" she was saying.

"I'm listening," said Kildare. "It's only that I'm trying to tell you that everything I want in the world will be lost if I don't turn in the report to the police."

"Ah, no, no! Don't say it!" cried Rosalie. "Because who'd talk? Who'd tell? Little Red is all man, clean through. And would *I* be making talk out of it? There's no one would know. And you'd be doing such a beautiful, secret thing that it would make God himself happy. And I'd be on my knees to you all the days of my life."

"I wish you weren't crying," said Kildare, sadly.

The tears came pouring, faster than ever; and yet it was very strange, he thought, that there was no distortion of the features, as from sobbing, but only a flush and a brightening that made her more lovely.

It seemed to him that the word lost out of his life until this moment was beauty—beauty which the eyes can taste and the soul possess for ever.

"I'm sorry; I'm so sorry!" she said. "I know what a man like you thinks of silly, crying women." She was opening a purse that had an enamel clasp as bright as a peacock moth and found a handkerchief within it. All the while, that fragrance which surrounded her rose upwards into his brain.

It was at this moment that he heard the unmistakable sound of a fall, a cry in Red's shrill voice, and a groan on a deeper note.

He ran out into the cellar corridor and saw Nick lying stretched along the floor, motionless, and Red on his knees by the body.

It had been a bad shock but there still was life in Nick. The first touch of Kildare's hand found it and he looked up with the reassuring word to Rosalie. She had altered very much from the instant before. Fear had given her quick, bright, calculating eyes like those of an animal.

"What happened?" she asked Red. "How did you dare to let him up . . . how did you dare!"

"He come alive," said Red, retreating a little, "and heard the two of you talking. He says that he won't be the ruining of a good guy like the doc; and me giving him a hand, he can get down to the docks and hide out there. And so I give him a hand and he gets along pretty good but the first step he takes on the stairs he goes slump; and the weight of him smacks me down. Doc, I ain't done him in, have I? I couldn't help letting him down. I wasn't braced, sort of."

Kildare picked Nick up and carried him back to the mattress. His pulse was fair but there was no doubt now that a blood transfusion was needed. The prick of the needle when he took a blood sample made the boy murmur but he lapsed into unconsciousness again.

"Stay here with him," he said to the girl. "You get

74

him a container of hot milk and coffee and keep him warm."

Red said: "Are you gonna turn him in, doc?"

"It's my duty," said Kildare, and hurried out of the house. The girl had followed him noiselessly to the cellar entrance beneath the porch. He turned back to her.

"Well?" he asked, sharply.

"Nothing. I'm not begging you, doctor," said Rosalie.

"It's a hospital case for a blood transfusion."

She was silent. Words could not have said so much.

The cold, blind rain beat swiftly against his face. Then he said to her, almost angrily: "You don't know what they'd do. They'd smash me flat. It's gaol for a doctor who works outside the law."

"I know," she said. She leaned weakly back against the wall and looked up at him, awaiting the final judgement, making no appeal.

"I'm going now," said Kildare.

"Yes, doctor," said the girl.

As he turned away, he still expected some outcry. That was why he made the first steps so slowly. But she did not speak. He even glanced over his shoulder, as he got to the sidewalk but she remained half seen in the shadow without making a sign. He turned into the sweep of rain and went on, walking fast, holding the grip of his emergency bag so hard that it hurt the palm of his hand. The thought of her kept pace with him.

When he got to the dispensary Probationer Mary Lamont stood up and looked at him without a smile.

"Anybody been in since I left?" he asked.

"Let's see—that was forty minutes ago, wasn't it?" she answered. "No. No one has been in."

Forty minutes! Into another world and back in forty minutes! That was how the sun stood still, then, that day over ancient Palestine.

"Take this blood sample to the hospital, type it," said Kildare, "and get me five hundred cc.'s of the correct type; then bring back the instruments for a blood transfusion, some citrate and the rest, please."

He wrote out the requisition hastily on an order blank, and gave it to her.

"If they ask the name of the patient and the location of the case, doctor —?" she asked.

"Perhaps they won't ask those questions," he answered. "Hurry, please."

Then he went through the side door to Sullivan's Saloon. He noticed that the end of the bar where he generally stood, was occupied. The voice of the bartender sang out at once: "Hey, Patsy, will you be backin' out of that stall and leave it for a better man than you?"

"What better man?" demanded Patsy. "And if he's bigger than me, how d'you know that I can't whittle him down to my own size?"

"Listen to the Irishman!" Mike chuckled. "The faces of Irishmen is flat because they're wore off by the fists of the whole world."

"Keep your place, Patsy," said Kildare. "The beer is as good down here as it is up there."

But Patsy came and took him by the arm.

"I worked for the Houlihan stables," he said, "and I

know that a horse feeds better out of his own manger. Come up here and take this place, Doctor Kildare. Mike, the drink's on me."

"And when would I be charging the doctor for a drink?" asked Mike.

He put the glass before Kildare, the fine foam neatly ruled off the top of it. Under his voice he said: "I've heard your bad news in the hospital, doc. You're too good for that old fool of a Gillespie. He's been a great man but the day has gone out of him and he's left in the dark."

"Be still, Mike," said Kildare. "You're talking of something you don't know."

"Ah, is it that way?" said Mike. "Well, it's a hard, hard thing to forgive a man that's wronged you."

"I've not been wronged, Mike."

"No? Well, it's you that say it. And after St. Patrick there was no snakes left in Ireland. So here's to you, doc!"

He finished that enigmatic speech by tossing off a quick shot of bar whisky.

Kildare, his beer finished, went back into the dispensary; and sat down to the thought of the dark cellar, the flaming head of the boy Red, Nick's white face, stiff with pain and the enduring of it. But when it came to Rosalie he felt that he must see her again before he could know her features. What he had from her was not a visual image but an intangible emotion such as music gives us when the pleasure is remembered but the notes forgotten.

The doorbell of the dispensary rang and he looked up

77

to see Mary Lamont entering. He said: "You didn't bring —anything?"

She was in distress, but she was calm and straightforward. He could see that she was like something out of a book—an old-fashioned book. You would not have to turn the page to know what happened, for the right would be sure to win. She was made all of one substance of social good and purity and truth.

All the morality of a copybook, he was sure, could be found in Mary Lamont, word for word, neatly embossed. No doubt she was intelligent, patient, careful, thrifty, hard-working, loyal, clean of heart.

She had beauty as well. A teacher of physiology could have touched Mary Lamont with a rubber-tipped pointer and said: "This is a correct hand; this is a correct foot; in this manner the ankle joint should be fitted; observe how the neck joins the shoulders and see how the head sits upon the neck; this is the forehead of *homo sapiens*; these deep-set eyes indicate the brainspace above them; observe the nobility of nose and mouth and chin; the example being female, the throat is soft."

But what of it? Who could give a second thought or glance to her after looking once into the soul of a Rosalie, that fourth dimensional creature of warmth and timeless spirit, who remained lovely in spite of tears?

So he watched, cold with thought, while the girl explained: "I tried to get in without being noticed, so I took the ambulance court...."

"But why?" asked Kildare.

"Because I was afraid that there might be questions

unless I could get directly to the man in charge of the storage blood and give him your requisition. But Miss Cavendish saw me. . . ."

"The fat woman?"

"Yes, doctor. She asked me if the dispensary had been closed as early as this. She wanted to know whether we were not keeping the usual hours."

"Ha? Ugly, was she?"

"Not ugly, but suspicious."

"What made her suspicious?"

"I think she was born that way."

"And then?"

"I told her that I'd only come over for a moment. She asked me what I had come for."

Here Mary Lamont paused. Her eyes asked him to complete the story.

"So, of course, you told her a white lie," said Kildare. "You made up a little story about something or other, so that you could get past her, didn't you?"

"No, doctor," said Mary Lamont.

"No, of course, you had to tell the truth. You always tell the truth, Miss Lamont, don't you?"

She was wretchedly silent. Her face began to colour but she kept looking him in the eye.

"Always the truth," said Kildare, ironically. "Even if it were a matter of life or death?"

"I guessed that it was life or death."

"But naturally you preferred death for the poor devil as long as you kept your own mouth clean?"

She was silent again. This cruel dropping of the acid

tormented her but she kept setting her teeth to keep from showing the pain.

"You'll be a good mother," said Kildare. "The doctor will tell you that you've been a brave little woman, whether the child lives or dies."

He stood up.

"I'm sorry, doctor," whispered the girl.

"You're what?" snapped Kildare. "Never mind. What happened after Cavendish talked to you?"

"When I couldn't give her the name of the patient or the address, she took me to Dr. Gillespie."

"Gillespie?" said Kildare, startled. "I'm not working under him any longer."

"No, doctor. But Dr. Gillespie started the out-patient system and he keeps in touch with everything that happens. He seemed angry."

"He didn't swear, did he?"

"Yes, doctor, a great deal."

"Odd," said Kildare, sneering. "He said that I could be damned before I got blood and instruments for a transfusion for an unnamed case. Was that what he said?"

"In general, yes, doctor."

She was silent. He went into the back room and picked up a few things. He came back and showed them.

"I must not do anything behind your back," he said. "You'll observe with your usual accuracy that I'm taking a coil of rubber tubing, a fifty cc. syringe, some sodium citrate, an Erlenmeyer flask, and other things. When Gillespie asks questions, I want you to be able to tell him everything."

80

Her head bowed. Suddenly he knew that she was close to tears. "I'm being a swine to you. I'm sorry," said Kildare.

She managed to get her head up and looked straight before her with blind, misted eyes. "No, doctor. It's all right."

Kildare said, softly, taking the words right out of his heart: "You know, when a fellow is in great pain he forgets the feelings of other people. I won't be this way again."

"Thank you, doctor. I understand," she answered.

"Do you?" said Kildare. "I wonder."

IX

LIFE FOR A LIFE

He went out into the rain, hurrying. The wind had come up. It gathered the dust of the falling rain and blew the thin spray into Kildare's face. He felt that he was taking his last walk through the world as he had known it. Tomorrow might bring a new existence. He wondered what life would be like without test tubes and microscopes and the faces of the sick.

When he came to the vacant house, he found a small, skulking figure under the porch. Red said: "He looks terrible bad."

Kildare said nothing. He lighted his way down the stairs with his torch. When he came to the door he shone the light inside, the ray cutting sharply through the yellow glow of the lantern, showing him Rosalie's terrified face. She had her hands up as though she were trying to turn the force of an impending blow.

Then she cried out: "Nick. Nick! It's not the police. He's come alone."

He leaned over Nick. The boy was far gone. He was ashen-grey. He looked like a death mask of the face Kildare had first seen.

He got his eyes open, one wider than the other. "Hi, doc," he said, faintly.

"Hi, Nick."

Looking down at what might be his last case, he had a queer feeling that he was giving a life for a life. The law would strike him down for it, but the law was a fool.

"You didn't tell them?" asked Nick.

"Be still."

"Okay," Nick whispered.

The girl was smiling a little, also, but always with the look of one asking permission.

Kildare turned to Red. "Would you give some of your blood to this fellow, Red?" he asked.

"Wouldn't I just!" said Red, and came a step out of his corner.

"You've got to have a blood transfusion," said Kildare to Nick. "There are four types of blood. If one of us has the right type we can put the life back inside of you. Your sister is the best bet, so we'll begin with her."

He had in his bag a physiological solution of salt and water, a teaspoonful to a pint. Into each of three tubes he put a measured bit of this; from the girl, from Red, and from his own finger he took drops of blood and placed them in the test tubes with the solution. He took more blood from Nick and watched the straw-coloured serum of it form in the bottom of another test tube.

There was needed endless time for this. Now and then he took Nick's pulse, but the boy's look as life ebbed in him was enough. No one tried to be cheerful, but Rosalie sat down beside Nick and put a hand on his forehead.

His eyes kept following Kildare around the room, but he said to his sister: "Sing something, will you?"

She sang. She seemed unable to remember the words, so she filled in by chanting: "*Ta da-ta da—ta dum.*" She tried snatches of jazz; she got down to Mother Goose, but somehow she managed to keep a song in the air.

"You got a rotten memory," said Nick, once.

"I'm sorry. I know I'm no good," said Rosalie. "I'm *so* sorry, honey."

"No, you're okay," murmured Nick. "You keep me from thinking about myself."

She sang and sang, and her singing drew them all together.

Kildare was ready for the next step. He needed a shallow, clear dish. The crystal from his watch would serve. He put the girl's blood cells from the salt solution with the drops of mixed blood serum in the crystal and held the light of the electric flash under the tiny dish while he watched for signs of grouping.

Gradually minute yellowish drops appeared in the solution.

He shook the drops of serum out on the floor and said to the three intent faces: "She's no good for Nick."

"But I've got to be right for him!" cried Rosalie.

"Shut up, Rosalie!" Red snapped, keeping his eyes on Kildare as though he were reading marvels from a strange book.

The same agglutination formed when Red's blood was tried. Again Kildare emptied the tiny dish and used his own serum. When he shook the drops together they mixed perfectly. The strong light from the electric torch showed not the slightest agglutination. He looked up with a smile at Nick.

"It's all right, Nick," he said, nodding. "My blood will fit like nobody's business."

"But wait a minute," protested Nick. "You can't do that—I mean, you can't give me—it's not right!"

"Hush, Nick," said the girl, strangely breathless.

"I mean," said Nick through his teeth to her, as she leaned over him, "suppose that something happened to him *after* he'd put his own blood inside me. D'you see now?"

It was as though a mystic importance, a sort of blood-brotherhood, must underlie the transfusion. Kildare had started boiling the instruments over a fire. It was a full dish so that the boiling had taken longer. The Erlenmeyer flask, rubber and glass tubing, cork, needles, and the big syringe all simmered together.

He cut another length of the rubber tubing and applied it as a tourniquet about his left arm after he had set up the flask and put into it the contents of some small ampules of citrate solution.

When the tourniquet had taken a good grip and the veins were standing out close to the bend of the arm, he thrust in a big needle and let the blood flow down the tubing into the flask. Nick, who had endured seeing whole oceans of his own blood, could not quite go that needle-dig. He had to put a shaky hand over his eyes; but Rosalie, bright as a bird, watched everything.

85

Kildare said: "Take the bottle and keep shaking it, Red, will you? We can't let the blood coagulate."

"I can't do it," said Red, his hand shrinking away from the filling bottle. "I'm sorry, doc, but it makes me kind of sick."

"I'll do it," said the girl, and picking up the bottle she kept it in steady motion. She did not change colour. She only said: "Does it make you a little dizzy to lose so much? Will it be all right for you, doc?"

"To lose a pint? Of course it will," smiled Kildare, yet he was feeling a small, insistent pull on his strength.

He heard Nick whispering to Red: "But takin' the life right out of his body into mine . . ."

"Yeah, I know," said Red.

"It'll change me, maybe," said Nick.

It was a quart bottle and Kildare filled it more than half full. Then he removed the needle, stopped the bleeding, and took off the tourniquet. After that he took a sterile needle and jabbed it into a vein on the arm of Nick.

Nick moved his head and looked at the wall, refusing to watch as Kildare held up the bottle and let the blood slowly seep down into Nick's body.

It was different with the girl. She sat against the wall and kept her eyes fixed not on Kildare, but on the operation. While the blood ran, her eyes widened and fixed. Her lips parted; her head bent back a little; and as the colour drained out of her face, it seemed that she was giving Nick life out of her own body. Kildare had watched a thousand transfusions, but now it was as though the operation were being performed for the first time, following it with Rosalie's eyes.

He removed the needle from Nick and cleaned the apparatus with alcohol.

Red came back from his corner stealthily to whisper: "Nick, are you okay now? You got a colour back in your face. You look swell, Nick."

"Sure, I'm okay, now."

The girl was still sitting back against the wall holding her brother's free hand. She was pale and her lowered eyes showed a blue stain across the lids.

"How you feeling, Nick?" asked Kildare.

The boy looked up at the ceiling, not at the doctor. Gradually he forced his glance to meet Kildare's. "I could eat a horse," he said, "and drink a whole keg of beer."

"You're going to sleep first," smiled Kildare.

"Okay, doc," agreed Nick. "Anything you say."

"I'm jabbing another needle into you," said Kildare. "It'll bring that sleep along a little faster."

"Go as far as you like." Nick grinned and held out his arm. He smiled at the twinge of the injection.

"Is the pain in your breast getting bad?" asked Kildare.

"It's sinking a tooth in me, but it's all right. Everything's all right," said Nick.

"How about *you*? You look knocked out," said Kildare to the girl.

She reacted to his voice as though she were awakening from a profound sleep. Her eyes opened wide like the eyes of a child; and with a child's immense seriousness she looked at him.

"I'm all right," she whispered, and gradually her smile commenced. Kildare watched it grow.

Later, with his instruments repacked, Kildare stood by Nick and watched him in fast sleep with one arm thrown above his head.

Red twitched his coat sleeve. "Go on, doc," he advised. "Get out of here before the cops know you've been in on this deal and hang a rap on you."

"I'm going," agreed Kildare. "So long, Red. Good-bye, Rosalie."

"I'm coming out," she said, and she walked silently with him from the cellar to the entrance beneath the porch of the house.

The rain was coming down crash; the pavement shone with the bright dust of it under the street lamps.

"I've got a car around the corner," said Rosalie. "I'll drive you back to the hospital."

"It's only two or three blocks," protested Kildare.

"I know, but I'm taking you," she insisted.

There was no strength in him for argument. He was so done in that his knees were uncertain beneath his weight. So he climbed after her into a small coupé. He could not help thinking that it was a little odd that she should have a car of her own; it went with something expensively modish about the cut of her clothes.

He was glad she did not talk. Presently the car stopped and he saw her getting out. She ran through the rain into a little corner café. He wondered after her, vaguely and pleasantly, and then she was out again and beside him with a big cup of coffee.

"Why—thanks a lot," said Kildare, a little amazed.

"Hush! You don't have to talk."

It was not the finest coffee in the world but into the aroma of it passed a slight breath of that perfume which Rosalie was wearing. The bitterness and the heat comforted his very heart. She lighted a cigarette and passed it to him.

He took the smoke in deep breaths. It was almost gone before he had finished the coffee; and now as he pushed the door open to return the cup, he found it taken firmly from his hand. She was running through the rain again into the café, and out and into the car. Her tweed coat was moist enough to give a pleasant outdoor odour and the furpiece ruffed up around her throat a thousand glittering little jewel points. He took a lazy note of her and closed his eyes again.

Presently the car was making speed and on either side he heard tyres ripping and whirling over wet pavement. He opened his eyes and found that they were curving up through Central Park.

"But wait a minute, Rosalie," he said. "I ought to get back to the dispensary. I'm late."

There was something different about her. Perhaps it was because she had taken off her hat and tossed it into the space behind the seat. It gave her head a new and softer outline, and perhaps it was this that seemed to lend her a different meaning.

"You'll be back before long," she said, and leaning across him she twisted open the small ventilator at his side.

"Get some of that in your face."

He put back his head again. A foolish weakness in his face kept him smiling a little no matter what he did to stop it. The world of serious care remained far behind them, and every spin of the wheels carried them farther and farther away from it.

"There's a quiet place ahead where we can sit and talk," said Rosalie. "I have to say something, and Nick will be all right, won't he? Red won't leave him."

Kildare nodded. He kept his eyes half open. Through the coursing water on the windshield, he looked out at a drowned world, an infinitely involved pattern of crimson and gold and purple which took on, in the distance, and in the night, a general tone of bronze.

Presently the car pulled up near the edge of a pond. The headlights showed an open boat with the rain beating ceaselessly down upon it. She switched them off. The lake remained visible in the light of the myriad rain-splashes on its surface. A tree, which held its branches over them, kept the downpour from rattling like stones on the roof of the car.

"Now," said the girl, "we can talk about Nick. I want to tell you everything I know about it, so that you'll see what you've done. But now that the job is finished, the law will never be able to touch you. You'll be all right, won't you?"

"He still needs a doctor's care," said Kildare.

"I won't let you go near him again!" cried Rosalie.

"Won't let me?" he repeated. He laughed a little weakly. "She won't let me!" he murmured, and he closed his eyes. "Tell me how you'll keep me away."

He waited for an answer until the pause troubled him and he cast about in his mind for a way of reopening the conversation. Sleepiness dimmed the world and thrust away the illumined fairyland of Central Park South.

It seemed to him that he was saying something about them, and then he wakened with knowledge, like a shadowy handstroke past his face, that much time had passed. Even that alarm did not rouse him to complete consciousness at a stroke, but by degrees he passed out of the world of his sleep. And every wind that blew in that other universe carried the fragrance of that perfume of Rosalie's.

His face was pillowed in fur. He had sideslipped in the seat and Rosalie had given his head a place on her shoulder.

"I'm sorry," said Kildare, starting up. "I'm terribly sorry."

"Are you?" asked Rosalie.

"I mean you wanted to talk . . ." said Kildare.

"It was better than talk," said Rosalie. "It was lovely."

She had a dreaming softness of voice and Kildare, peering with clouded eyes, saw that she was smiling to herself. Her head lay back against the top of the seat and her half-opened eyes regarded the lights over the lake.

Something was lacking from the world as it had been before he fell asleep. He could not tell what the change had been; he was puzzled and confused, trying to find it.

He leaned forward a little, trying to understand her

smile, which troubled him. The girl, staring, seemed un-
aware of his gaze. Suddenly he realised that she was
seeing him with her mind's eye. He spoke her name,
quietly, and gradually her eyes turned to include him in
her dream.

He lifted her hand, palm up, and kissed it. The soft tips
of her fingers touched his face and held to it lightly.

X

INQUISITION

Mary Lamont had waited a full hour after the time for closing the dispensary. She had cleaned and re-cleaned everything and at last a telephone call from the hospital wanted to know whether or not Doctor James Kildare intended to bestow his services upon the district all night or if he would kindly return to resume his duties.

She switched off the lights. The radiance from the street printed a black pattern on the inner wall; and something ghostly, out of the past, closed in around her. There are moments which soil the spirit as soot dirties the hands.

She stepped out, turned the key in the lock, and went back towards the hospital, wondering what questions she would have to answer.

The front entrance was the nearest, but for some reason she went around to the south side. That was why she happened to see young Doctor Kildare getting out of a little coupé, and standing beside it saying good-bye. She saw held out to him a woman's hand with the wink of a jewel on it like a cat's eye in the dark. The girl in the car was like something seen under water. Mary made a visual effort that caused the optic nerve to ache all the way to her heart, as she grew aware of the fox fur and the pretty face above it.

Mary Lamont, taking note of these things with that power of observation which Kildare had praised, could not fail to notice at the same time how long the young doctor held the girl's hand and how he looked after the car as it moved away.

She checked in her name at the desk as she entered. "Lamont? Wait a minute," said the girl at the desk. "Doctor Gillespie wants you to report to him. Oh, Doctor Kildare, you're wanted by Doctor Carew."

Kildare nodded at Mary Lamont. He had the look of one who has visited "fresh woods and pastures new," a far-off eye as though in thought he still wandered through them.

"I waited till an hour after closing time for the dispensary," said the girl, "and then there was a call from the hospital."

"An hour after? Am I late?" asked Kildare, vaguely. He looked up at the big clock on the wall, but he did not seem greatly alarmed. He even yawned and smiled a little under the nurse's eye. "Some of the instruments need to be cleaned. Will you boil them up for me?" he asked, giving her the emergency bag.

Then he was gone down the hall with an easy saunter as though a call from the grim head of the hospital was a small thing in his life. Mary Lamont looked after him a moment, weighing the bag thoughtfully in her hand, then she went straight to Gillespie.

She was admitted at once, in time to hear him saying

to a little old blue-eyed lady: "Plenty of rest—no hasty motions—up the stairs one step at a time."

As the old woman went from the room, Gillespie gave his wheelchair a hitch that jerked it violently around.

"An hour late, eh?" he said. "Why?"

"I had to wait for orders to close the dispensary, doctor."

"Let me see. You're the nurse that smiles, aren't you?"

"Sometimes, doctor."

"You're not smiling now. What's the matter?"

"Nothing, sir."

"Kildare didn't show up at the dispensary, eh? You had to get orders directly from the hospital?"

She was silent.

"I don't give a continental damn about Kildare," said Gillespie, "but the weight of that infernal dispensary system is never off my shoulders and I'm going to see that it *works*! Where's this Kildare now?"

"He's in the hospital, doctor."

"Did you see him come in?"

"Yes, doctor."

"How did he come?"

"In an automobile, sir."

"Who brought him?"

"A woman was driving the car."

"He doesn't know any women!"

"She was extremely pretty," said Mary Lamont, her eyes wandering away to the memory. "She had bright hair ... quite beautiful."

"What sort of beauty?"

Mary Lamont recovered herself with a start. "I know nothing whatever about her."

"Don't tell me that," growled Gillespie. "Women know everything, particularly about other women. Where was Kildare?"

"I don't know, sir."

"What about that blood transfusion?"

"I was unable to bring him what he needed, doctor."

"Naturally. But did that stop him?"

"There was no blood from the hospital."

"I ask—did that stop him?"

"I don't see how he could have gone ahead, doctor."

"Oh, you don't, don't you? I want you to understand that that young fool sticks to what he wants to do. If he wanted to make a blood transfusion without instruments, he'd improvise them."

"But he didn't have the blood, doctor."

"He'd find it," stated Gillespie. "In a pinch he'd go out on the street, knock a man on the head and drag him in and steal the blood out of his veins. That's the sort of a bandit that wild young doctor is. He left the dispensary, eh?"

"Yes, doctor."

"You don't know where he went?"

"No, doctor."

"How long was he gone?"

She paused, frowning, uneasy. "I don't know—exactly."

"Who asked for exactness? Was he gone five minutes or an hour?"

She said slowly: "More than an hour."

"Ha!" exclaimed Gillespie. "And you don't know what he was doing?"

"No, doctor."

"Can't you guess?"

She hesitated and her colour rose.

Gillespie said suddenly: "What's that bag you've got there?"

"Doctor Kildare's," said the girl.

"Give it to me," said Gillespie. "I'll find the trail he's followed by the dirt on his shoes."

"Doctor Kildare told me to clean the instruments in the bag, doctor," she said.

"What good would they be to me after they're cleaned?" cried Gillespie. "Give me the lot the way they are."

She took a good breath.

"I'm sorry, doctor."

"Sorry for what?" snapped Gillespie.

"I'm a nurse, sir, not a spy," she told him.

"Oh, a nurse, are you?" asked Gillespie. "A nurse that can't do what you're told? What sort of a nurse is that?"

She was silent. He lowered his voice to say: "I'm definitely ordering you to give me that emergency bag."

"With Doctor Kildare's permission?" she asked.

"The devil take Kildare and his permission!" said Gillespie. "How can a half-baked young cub of an intern give me any sort of a permission? Are you defying me? I think you are, to my face."

She was badly frightened but she held her head up and, as her unfailing custom was in the tight spots, she kept looking Gillespie straight in the eye. She could only falter: "These are Doctor Kildare's personal possessions, sir."

"Damn his personal possessions; and take yourself out of my sight," said Gillespie.

She got with some dignity to the door, but he saw the white of her face as she escaped through it. He was calling out, at the same time: "Get Cavendish. Get her on the run!" Then he swept up the telephone to bellow: "Give me Carew! That you, Carew? Have you had your hands on Kildare, yet? When you tackle him, find out what he did when he was away from the dispensary this afternoon. Don't stop massaging him till you get the information. Next patient!"

He had dropped the telephone as he spoke, and as usual it toppled over.

As the door opened and the next patient appeared, he shouted at his nurse: "Keep them out of here till I ask for them!"

"But you just asked for one, doctor," said the trembling nurse.

"Did nothing of the kind," said Gillespie. "Don't start telling me what's in my mind. Keep 'em out!"

A moment later the door opened again.

"Stay out!" called Gillespie before the billowing form of Molly Cavendish had fully appeared.

"Gladly," said the fat nurse, beginning to vanish.

"Come here—Cavendish! Come here!" he commanded.

She stepped inside and closed the door.

"This hospital is nothing but a damned wreck and

riot!" declared Gillespie. "I thought you were supposed to keep an eye on the nurses?"

"I keep an eye on them when I can," she said, "but I'm dragged off duty by a bad-tempered old man who lives on nothing but trouble. What's wrong with you now?"

"A little nineteen-year-old green-eyed slip of nothing comes in here and defies me to my face!" growled Gillespie. "Why did you ever pick her out in the first place?"

"I didn't," said Cavendish. "She was only one of three."

"You sent her sandwiched between a shrew and a damned fool," said the doctor, "so I only had one choice. You meant me to choose her from the first."

"If she won't do, fire her," suggested the nurse. "You're good at firing."

"Change horses in the middle of the stream? I'm not a half-wit, am I?"

Cavendish was silent.

"Am I?" cried Gillespie.

"I can't say, off-hand," she replied.

"They learn their stubbornness from you," said Gillespie. "You go around the hospital sowing the seeds of revolt. Molly, are you close to this Lamont girl?"

"I've told her to give up nursing; I've told her that she's too fine for this dirty work," said Cavendish. "I'm that close to her."

"Get closer still," directed Gillespie. "Our little game is working, old girl, but only half-way, and the wrong half at that."

"What game?" asked Cavendish.

99

"Kildare and the probationer."

"I've nothing to do with any sort of a game," said Molly.

"It was your own suggestion," said Gillespie.

"That's not true."

"Don't try to lie out of it. If you'd picked out a girl with a brain it would have been all right, but the silly little fool is falling in love with him."

"Naturally," said Molly.

"Why naturally?"

"She won't be the last."

"You mean that he plays fast and loose with 'em?"

"That poor boy?"

"Then what the devil are you talking about? I say that the young idiot is running around after a red-headed rat of a little chorus girl."

"How do you know?" asked Molly.

"By the way the Lamont girl spoke of her. The right sort of female can tell the wrong kind a mile off. . . . Find out everything that's known about the redhead. You hear?"

"Do you think that I never get tired of you and your dirty work?"

"You get tired of me but not of my dirty work. Molly, be a sweet mother confessor to this Lamont creature. Make her empty her heart for you. Find out from her where Kildare was this afternoon. Let her tell you just how much Kildare means to her."

"I thought you were through with Kildare," said Molly.

"I've fired him, haven't I?" asked Gillespie.

"So that he could get experience—yes. Now he's out getting it and you begin to howl like a sick baby."

"Don't you understand that when it comes to women any young man is never more than two steps from hell?"

"And what about the women?"

"Women? They don't count," he answered violently. "There's enough and to burn of them. Be off and stop bothering me now. Do you think that I can waste my whole day gossiping here with you?"

XI

ULTIMATUM AND CHORALE

The great Carew, who had nursed the hospital from sickly infancy to a gigantic maturity, put his elbow on his desk, his chin on his fist, and stared for a moment at Kildare. He said: "Young man, you have returned from the dispensary more than an hour late. What were you doing during that time?"

"During part of it I was asleep."

"Asleep? Asleep where, young man?"

"I can't tell you, sir," said Kildare.

"Cannot? That means, 'Will not!' You understand that hospital time is not your own? It must be accounted for?"

"I can account for every hour I've been in the hospital except for a part of this afternoon," answered Kildare.

He watched the wrath gather on the super's face.

"I am forced to demand, definitely demand, that you make the accounting of your time to me," said Carew.

Kildare was silent.

The superintendent continued: "You have been in a special position in this hospital as the assistant of Doctor Gillespie. I need not tell you that that special position no longer exists. It is my duty to see that you return to the full discipline which governs the actions of every other intern. We make no exceptions. Is that clear?"

"Yes, sir," said Kildare.

"You still persist in refusing to answer?"

"I'm sorry, sir."

"I may even conceive that in the future you might become still sorrier. However, I do not believe in hasty action. I am giving you twenty-four hours to consider. At that time I shall be ready to act!" said Carew. "You may go."

The quartet in Sullivan's Saloon was composed of Detective Flaherty, ambulance-driver Weyman from the hospital, Mike, and that red-nosed water-eyed Slip Ginnis. They used to gather in a close group, lean their heads together, and listen with vacant eyes to the Muse as they improvised their parts.

When someone fell too abysmally out of key and tune, three pairs of glowering eyes fixed instantly upon him; and he who produced an unexpected grace note or any sort of an agreeable flourish received smiles of affection. Once when Slip Ginnis brought forth a tenor note of youthful resonance, Mike set up the drinks for him through the whole evening. Music bound these four inseparably together and only death or a bad cold could cleave them asunder.

That was why melancholy came upon the saloon late one night. Ginnis was gone where beer chasers after rye whisky have driven better men; Detective Flaherty was called away on duty; and that left Weyman and Mike alone to carry on.

It was one in the morning, the night had been dull, and there was not another soul in the saloon on whom they could rely for an upper register in their songs. They had embarked on "John Peel", which was a poor selection, for the song never can have the proper swing and rhythm without a few high notes to carry it whooping along after the fox so gallantly. All that Weyman and Mike could do was to labour like two old cart horses, until from the corner they heard a rather husky baritone lift the entire song out of the ruck.

They turned and saw a white-haired old man who had just rolled his wheelchair in from the street.

"Mother above us!" said Mike. "It's the great Gillespie!"

Weyman was past speech and reached for the whisky which he dared not drink.

If the brightest archangel of all came down to earth, he would find a homely reception from the Irish, and the gift at least of the oldest pipe in the best chair nearest the kitchen stove.

Mike went forward to greet his distinguished visitor, but Gillespie, waving them back with a hand that kept time for the tune, rolled himself to the bar. He sang the song through to the end. Then he pulled himself out of the chair and grabbed the rail of the bar. Weyman tried to help him.

"Keep your hands off me," snapped Gillespie. "Tell him to leave me alone, Mike."

"Even as close as I am to the hospital, sir," said Mike, delighted, "I wouldn't of guessed that you knew my name, at all."

"What else do I hear from our young interns except what Mike says or doesn't say?" demanded Gillespie. "What have you got to drink, here?"

"A fine beer, sir."

"Beer is a good drink for a fat man on a hot day," said Gillespie. "But for those that are tough and lean and old it's nothing but water. There's no greeting in it. Give me a whisky, Mike."

They all laughed and Gillespie, tossing off the drink, struck into "Auld Lang Syne". They finished the song and another drink before Gillespie looked about to say: "It's a good cheerful room, Mike. I wouldn't have thought that young Kildare and some of the rest have started to skid here and gone all the way to the devil."

"Kildare? Kildare?" cried Weyman. "He's not gone to the devil, doctor!"

"Ah, but he has!" said Gillespie, shaking his head.

"He's as far from the devil as a full keg is from an empty one," said Mike. "He's a good friend to the two of us, doctor."

"Your friend?" repeated Gillespie, apparently much surprised.

"A friend when you need him, and that's the right kind," said Weyman.

"Yes," admitted Gillespie, "there was a time when I had a great hope for him, but, of course, that was before he began to go wrong."

"Go wrong?" cried the two.

"Better men than Jimmy Kildare have gone head-first to the devil because a pretty girl looked at them," said Gillespie. "So we won't blame him. We'll only pity him, boys, won't we?"

"I know him," said Weyman, "better than I know my own eye; and there's no women for him just now; he's married to his work, doctor."

"Come, come!" said Gillespie. "Why not be frank? It can't do him harm. He's no longer working for me. He's not my assistant now."

"If I thought," said Weyman, "that he was standing in the shade that any skirt in this district can throw, I'd tell you plain."

"Well, well," said the doctor, "let me have another drink and we'll say no more about it. Once they begin to slide, they're soon gone. I'm drinking to poor Jimmy Kildare. May the woman have joy of him, and God help him."

Weyman and Mike, staring at one another, allowed their drinks to rest untasted on the bar.

"Someone has lied to you, sir," said Weyman.

"Lies? Lies?" said the doctor. "I talk about what I've seen with my own eyes."

"You saw her," said Mike eagerly. "Is she enough to drive the doc out of his head?"

"If you saw her pretty face and her red hair, you'd understand it, Mike," said Gillespie.

"The redheads! The redheads!" Mike exclaimed. "That's the fire that's cooked many a man's dish for him. What's her name, doctor?"

"I can't tell you," said Gillespie. "But you're the man who knows everything in the district and you can find out about her if you want."

"I'll have her scalp!" said Weyman.

"You'll have Kildare at you if you do," said Gillespie. "But it's time for me to get back to work. Thanks for the drink. But the song was what did me good." And sitting down in the wheelchair, with an eye that defied Weyman to help him, he rolled out on to the street.

Weyman followed the great man a few helpless steps. When he turned towards the bar again, Mike pointed a finger at him, roaring:

"You're the fine friend, the good friend, the true friend!"

"Friend to what?"

"The best friend, the only friend in the world to you, was what he was. My God, is there no shame in you, Weyman? Is there no blush for your dirty face?"

"Are you blaming me for Kildare's redhead?" cried Weyman.

"Him that sees no wrong till the fist's in his face; him that asks no man for naught but gives the bottom penny out of his pants pocket; him that takes on the blame for the drunken hoodlums like Weyman; *him* you turn loose for the guttersnipes and the ragamuffins to lay on their hands and their eyes! My God, Weyman, remember it when you next see Father O'Toole!"

Between anger at Mike and fear for Kildare, Weyman was left helplessly stammering.

"She'll have him out of the hospital to polish her boots

for her," said Mike. "She'll tear his life up to tatters in her two hands and then throw the tatters away and laugh at him over her shoulder. You can see the poor boy is all heart and no sense, but you turn him loose on his own, and God forgive you!"

Weyman, his hands gripped close together, looked into infinite space. "I'll find her," he said. "And I'll change her mind unless I've lost my grip."

"I've little faith in you, Weyman. Whisky and singing and singing and whisky is all you're good for while the poor doc is going to the dogs!"

XII

REDHEAD

James Kildare did not see Gillespie again until the great man, accompanied by the noted brain-specialist, Dr. Lawrence Corbin, was making one of his dreaded tours of the wards, grunting at the progress of this case, raging against the persistent fever of another, pointing his gnarled forefinger at a terrified Italian whose mountainous belly loomed and trembled under the covers, and making life a scream of misery to every nurse and luckless intern who happened to be around.

By the time they had reached the farther end of the huge white-washed room, Gillespie had gathered in his wake three or four of the staff physicians, who followed his chair at what they hoped was a reasonably safe distance, their foreheads cut across by frowns of wincing apprehension.

Gillespie suddenly jerked his chair to a savage halt.

"Who's that over there—mooning by the window?" he demanded.

Somebody stammered that it was young Kildare.

"Get him here. Kildare! Kildare!" called Gillespie.

There was not a sign of response.

"He's in a day-dream. He thinks that he can't be

hearing human voices out of the deep blue sea. Go get him, one of you."

But Kildare now became aware of the attention focused on him. He turned slowly towards the group.

"Kildare, come here!" roared Gillespie.

Kildare obeyed at once. Gillespie crucified him from a distance with his pointing hand. "There's the man with the observing eye—there's the man with the medical memory. Aren't you, Kildare?"

"Nothing unusual, sir, I'm afraid," said Kildare.

"No? Nothing unusual?" asked Gillespie. "Then why the devil did you try to make yourself into a diagnostician?"

Kildare looked only at the old, leering, scowling face, aware of the expectant grins of the other doctors. Gillespie was hardly more famous for giving relief to the sick than he was for giving pain to the medical staff of the hospital. The dullness which routine produces, the humdrum stupidities of the average intelligence were to his electric mind intolerable evils and he tried continually to scourge them out of existence. It was a game which he always played though he knew that he never could win.

"Why didn't you tell me in the beginning," went on Gillespie, "that it was nonsense for me to try to teach you?"

"Perhaps," said Kildare, "I was a fool. But even a fool keeps hoping, I suppose."

Gillespie said to the group at large: "This fellow Kildare is going to become the Little Brother of Hell's Kitchen. He runs a dispensary just now, in the out-patient

110

department, and the good he can do at his office is not enough for him. He has to slip away, leaving a room full of children screaming with colic, old women groaning with sciatica, and heart cases gasping for breath—they're not enough for our very young Doctor Kildare—he has to sneak off into the shadows, somewhere, and pull more sick people out of ratholes, and treat them mysteriously, and fail to put their names on his reports.

"Our man of mystery. That's what he wants to become in Hell's Kitchen!"

The laughter of the others covered Kildare's silence. As he stood staring into the eyes of that malicious old man, he could not help remembering that just in this way, her face crimson, her eyes fixed immovably on his, his dispensary nurse had endured his ironical upbraiding. There was a certain bitter justice in the pain that was being meted out to him now and he recognised it.

"Run along, now, all of you," Gillespie growled. "Cavendish, what are you doing skulking in corners?"

She came slowly to him as the others moved away.

"Well, Molly?" he asked quietly.

"Are you trying to drive the poor young man out of his mind?" said the Cavendish.

"Out of his mind? Bah! If he has a mind, a bit of flogging will bring it to life; and if he hasn't it'll improve his circulation."

"Unless it breaks his heart," she suggested.

"That heart of his will never be broken—not by men," said the doctor. "Did you see how he held up his head and put out his chin? You can hit Kildare with words that are clubs, but you can never beat his eyes down. No, no, Molly, leave me to deal with the men. A deep spur never made a good horse swerve. Leave me to handle the men but tell me about the girl. Have you talked to her?"

"About the weather," said Molly.

"About the what?" cried Gillespie.

"It's all I could get out of her."

"Nonsense! Fat has got into your brain. D'you mean to say that you couldn't straighten her out? That she's too deep for you?"

"Any woman that's made up her mind can be too deep for the devil himself," said Molly.

"What's she made up her mind about?" asked the doctor.

"About Kildare."

"Is she in love with him?"

"I don't know. But he's holy ground and the public is not admitted."

"D'you mean that we'll get no more help from her?"

"She'll do no more spying, consciously or unconsciously," said Molly.

"With a pair of hands like yours, you ought to be able to break her in two and find what's written inside her."

"And how far did *you* get in the breaking of her?" demanded Molly.

"Ignorance and stubbornness; the whole damned country is full of youth and foolishness," said Gillespie.

Kildare, back in his room, walked up and down the floor for a time with an unopened letter from Beatrice Raymond in his hand. Tom Collins, his room mate, as long and thin

112

as the drink of the same name, sat with his arms wrapped around his knees. He followed the striding figure of his room mate with melancholy, affectionate eyes.

"Old Jimmy . . ." he said. "You don't have to keep smiling here. There's no audience for you to fool. It's Gillespie again, isn't it? Why can't the old devil leave you alone? He's smacked you down and thrown you out of your job with him. Isn't that enough to suit him?"

"You're wrong," said Kildare.

Tom Collins stared at him.

"Good God, are you going to keep on defending him?"

"He can't help turning sour when he sees me," said Kildare. "It reminds him of a hope that he had and how the hope went wrong. I try to keep out of his sight, but he finds me now and then."

"He'll burn an extra thousand years in hell for what he's doing to you," declared Tom Collins. "Read your letter and cheer up. Is it from that gal in the country? Where's her picture that used to stand on your chest of drawers?"

"Let me see," said Kildare. "Ah, here it is. It must have fallen down."

It had dropped behind the bureau to the floor. He replaced it, looked for a moment at the features of the photograph, and then slit the letter open.

Dear Jimmy:

Do you know how long it's been? More than six weeks. That's a lot, for me. Your time is all hitched together and flows along in big pieces; but my time is divided. Every morning there is a morning mail; every afternoon there's an afternoon mail to wait for, and after that there's a whole, dull evening and a long night before another chance will come to hear from you.

Do you understand how it is? Somehow I feel that I can't take it much longer. I know that you're worried because you haven't written. You want to make it a really good letter when you do sit down to it, and the right time never comes for that. You don't want to give pain and I know you hate yourself for being unkind to me.

The truth is, Jimmy dear, that I'm not very important to you. I rather inveigled you into this engagement of ours. I took such a hard hold on you that you scarcely could break away without being brutal, so you simply submitted.

It's so clear to me, now, that I'm giving you back to yourself and your work. I say to myself that one day some of the work will be behind you and then maybe I could mean more to you, if we're both free when that time comes. There isn't a tear on this page and there's not one on my face, either, so I suppose this is not going to be such a very great tragedy even to me. But it makes me feel terribly wise and mature and rather like a sainted martyr, or something.

Beatrice.

He folded the letter carefully and put it away. "That was another sock, wasn't it?" asked Tom Collins. "It's a funny thing about girls. They always trip a fellow when he's already falling over on his face."

Kildare went off to the dispensary with an added sense of loss. He could not help feeling that he had lost something of great price. However, the letter and the brutality of Gillespie that morning had served to focus his whole life like a burning-glass on a single obect. Whatever the state of flux in the rest of his world, there remained to him Rosalie. At the thought of her, he was able to put all unhappiness with a single great gesture behind him.

As he passed Sullivan's Saloon, Mike was getting a paper from the news-stand of Joe Garibaldi. The two of them saluted Kildare and looked after him as he entered the dispensary.

"Keep half an eye on that door, Joe, will you?" asked Mike. "And if a girl that's worth looking at, a redheaded girl, goes into the doc's place, get into the saloon and tell me as fast as you can."

"Sure," said Joe. "Redheads are easy to see."

In the dispensary the usual crowd of patients had not gathered, so that Kildare had time to say to Mary Lamont: "I suppose Gillespie asked for the usual report?"

"Yes," said the girl. "He wanted to know if you had left the dispensary."

"You couldn't lie about that, of course?" asked Kildare.

"I told him you had been away."

"And how long?"

"Yes."

"Any other details he wanted to know?"

"He wanted me to give him your emergency bag."

Kildare started. As he thought of what that bag

115

contained it seemed as though his entire conscience had been laid bare under that unfailing eye.

"So you turned it over to him, naturally?"

"My only orders from you were to clean the instruments, doctor."

"You mean you did *not* give him the bag?"

"No, doctor. The bag doesn't belong to the hospital."

"Wait a minute. Gillespie wouldn't let you get away with that. He had his hands on it, finally."

"No, doctor."

Kildare stared at her. She seemed to be having unusual difficulty in meeting his eye. It was almost as though he had caught her in the telling of a lie.

"You mean," said Kildare, slowly, "that you stood your ground against the great Gillespie?"

"I couldn't do what he wanted."

"That's the strangest thing I ever heard. Didn't he raise a pretty high wind?"

"Yes, doctor. By the way, I found this in your bag."

She offered him her handkerchief, which was twisted in a knot around some irregular, small, heavy object. He read the meaning of it with his surgeon's finger-tips before he undid the knot. Mary Lamont was suddenly busy cleaning the washbowl in the corner of the room.

He untied the handkerchief, therefore, and noted from it a thin delicacy of perfume. It had not the rich glamour of that scent which Rosalie wore; it was rather more like the fragrance which a fine soap leaves for a moment on the skin. Then he rolled out into the palm of his hand the misshapen bullet which he had taken from the body of

Nick. It seemed to him that he must have been without his wits when he left that thing in the bag.

"Do you know that bullet wounds have to be reported to the police?" he demanded.

She nodded. There was a misery in her eyes which he could not quite explain.

"If you keep quiet about this, there may be trouble even for you," he suggested.

"Trouble for me?" echoed the girl.

"Look—I want to tell you something."

"Yes, doctor?"

"You're tops. You knock the spots out of anything I ever heard of," said Kildare swiftly.

She was stunned by this outburst of approbation. He narrowed his eyes, looking at her and at his great new idea of her.

"You don't realise what you are. You think other people are the same, but they're not. One of these days," said Kildare, "I'm going to give you a pretty happy surprise. I'm going to introduce you to yourself."

They both laughed but not very much. Perhaps each of them welcomed the sudden clang of the dispensary door for in the moment of interval something had been born between them. They were embarrassed because they had no name for it. To each of them something had been added and yet nothing had been taken away.

Perhaps an hour after this, Joe Garibaldi came into the saloon and said to Mike: "There's a high-class redhead just stepped into the doc's place."

"How high?" asked Mike.

"As high as a goose hangs," said Joe.

Mike went to the telephone in the back room and rang the hospital. He got Weyman.

"Are you on or off?" asked Mike.

"I'm on but I could get relief," said Weyman.

"Hotfoot it over here; there's a high-stepping redhead has just strutted into the doc's place, and you and me are gunna give her the old eye."

Weyman came over on the run.

"We go around the street entrance," said Mike. "The doc is kind of touchy if we barge in the side-door during business hours."

So they went around and through the street entrance.

"You got dizzy and near passed out and I brought you in here," said Mike. "That's why we gotta see the doc."

"How you mean *I* got dizzy? About what I got dizzy?" asked Weyman.

There were half a dozen in the dispensary and in the rear room they could see a girl with red-golden hair talking to Kildare. Nurse Lamont was busy replacing a bandage that gave comfort to a sprained ankle.

"It's her!" said Mike, staring at the redhead.

"It's Rosalie!" said Weyman, agape.

"Is she gunna cost him plenty or is she gunna cost him plenty?" asked Mike.

"Look at her sink that smile into him; and look at him swaller it," observed Weyman.

"Look at the dummy tying up her finger for her," said Mike. "Like he was fooling anybody that had eyes."

118

"I waited for you last night," the girl was saying to Kildare. "I waited and waited and you didn't come."

"I'm sorry," said Kildare. "I couldn't get away. . . . How's Nick?"

"He's hungry to see you. He loves you, Jimmy. He looks up so high to you that he can't find the right words to talk about you."

"We've got to get him out of that cellar before long," said Kildare, "and yet he seems to be doing pretty well even in that hole. Will you be there tonight? At seven, say, Rosalie?"

"I'll be there. And then you're coming home with me to my place, Jimmy, and have supper. I'm going to cook you a steak."

"How do you cook a steak?"

"The way cannibals love it," said Rosalie. "And I'm going to tell you all my plans; I've got a thousand plans. . . . Do I have to go?"

"Yes," said Kildare.

"Say something that'll make me go."

"Get out of my sight," quoted Kildare.

"I love it," said Rosalie. "Will you be with Nick at seven?"

"I'll be there."

"I won't have to wait a single minute?"

"Not half a minute."

"It was frightful last night. I kept thinking that something had happened. You won't let anything happen to you, will you, Jimmy? I mean, nothing except beautiful things, will you? Good-bye—darling!"

She went out through the waiting-room with Kildare behind her saying: "Next patient, please!" and as she went she became aware of the eyes of the nurse, slightly askance.

"Thank you *so* much," said Rosalie, glancing down at the bandage which encircled one finger.

"I hope the doctor put you out of pain?" said Nurse Lamont.

"You hope he did what?" repeated Rosalie, a little startled. Then she laughed and said: "Good-bye, Miss Lamont."

XIII

AT HEADQUARTERS

She went out thoughtfully, there had been such innuendo in the grave eyes of the nurse.

When she reached the street, red-faced Mike stepped up and walked beside her down the block.

"Hi, Mike," she said. "How's everything?"

"Listen, sister," said Mike, "I wanta tell you something."

"Politics?" asked Rosalie.

"Yeah. Lay off the doc."

She stopped. She looked hard at Mike. "I saw you snooping in the dispensary," she said. "Did you see enough?"

"I saw plenty," said Mike. "And now I'm telling you. Lay off!"

"Or what?"

"Sullivan could tell you what."

"You wouldn't sic big Sullivan on a poor girl like me, would you?" asked Rosalie.

"Don't be hard, Rosalie. You can't be hard with me. I know too much about you."

"So what?"

"What d'you want out of the old doc?"

"I had a bad finger," she said, showing the bandage.

"Like hell. What you want out of the doc?"

"Who's he but a poor little intern without a bean in the world?"

"Yeah?" said Mike. "They're getting to know that guy around here. You take and ask around through the district and they'll tell you what kind of man he is. But you don't have to be told. You know too well."

"Oh, do I?"

"Yeah, you do. You know what he is, and you want it."

"You're talking crazy," said the girl.

"You got an idea about him. You got a marrying idea."

"I haven't anything of the kind. Anyway, it's none of your . . . Mike, I haven't anything of the kind. And what are you trying to do to me?"

"Quit it," said Mike. "Don't pull the waterworks on me."

"I'm not going to cry, Mike," said the girl. "But I wish you'd give me a chance to tell you something."

"That's what I want. I want you to tell me plenty. I want you to tell me, does the doc know about you?"

"What you mean?" asked Rosalie.

"You know what I mean, all right," said Mike.

"Will you let me talk to you?"

"What's keeping you back?"

"Mike, will you come in and have a drink on me in Pete's place?"

122

"What's the matter with talking out here?"

"Mike, give me a chance, will you?"

"You can have your chance right here and now. Talk up. Does Kildare know about all those others?"

"I've been talked about but I haven't been so really bad."

"Where'd you get that chunk of fur around your neck?"

"It's more than a year old, almost. Mike, please!"

"Sure I'll please," said Mike, "when you take and lay off of the doc."

"Will you let me try to tell you? It isn't anything bad I want from him. He hasn't any money."

"Yeah, that's what almost stops me."

She seized on this opening, this instant of his weakness, and rushed on: "You see, I can't get anything from him. I can only give. I'm going to give and give."

"Yeah, like hell."

"I mean, I really will. I'll read books and things. I'll practise up to be a nurse. Look, Mike, I can cook and I can sew. My mother taught me."

"What else did your mother teach you? Rosalie, he's just a damn young fool. He don't know anything. He thinks everybody that smiles is a nice guy and the ones that don't smile, they're sick and he'll help them."

"I know," said Rosalie.

"It wouldn't be any good, anyway. If you got your hands on him, Weyman—you know Weyman, don't you?"

"Yeah, I know him."

"Kid, if you laid a hold on the doc, Weyman would go crazy. He'd come and break you in two."

"I know," said Rosalie.

"Are you sick?"

"Yeah. I'm terribly sick."

"Lean on me and walk slow. I'm sorry for you, Rosalie. But when I next see the doc, I'm gunna tell him all about you."

"No!"

"What's the difference? He's bound to find out, some-time."

"After I've got him. I'm going to love him so's he'll never be able to give me up. He'll never be happy without me."

"Maybe you're right," said Mike. "But it's better for him to have the heart broke inside him than be saddled with you."

"Why do you say that? Don't you think I can change?"

"Yeah. Sure. The way a dope changes. I know you and I know your kind. You can turn yourselves into angels for a year or two and then you crack up. You won't crack alone. But you're not cracking Kildare with you."

"No," she said, suddenly past argument. "But ah, Mike, it hurts me clear to my heart. Listen to me, will you? Mike, suppose I don't marry him. Then there won't be anything to hold him to me. That would be all right, wouldn't it?"

"It sounds all right, but it wouldn't do."

124

"Nobody would talk about us. Every human being that watched us together would see how I loved him, and there wouldn't be any talk. Just for a little while —"

"Look, Rosalie. I'll tell you the straight of it. It's all that I'm gunna say before I go straight to the doc and tell him everything I know about you. If he ever started with you he'd never give you up. You know that."

"I don't know it, Mike. Please!"

"You *do* know it, right down in your heart. When you hit the skids he'd hit them too, trying to save you. I've seen his kind, here and there. There ain't many of them but I've seen the type. The honourable damn fools, is what I mean."

"Mike, give me a chance, will you?"

"Let go!"

Doctor Gillespie said: "Who's Weyman? What? An ambulance-driver? I don't want an ambulance . . . Wait a minute. Now I remember. Let him come in, will you?"

The nurse sent in Weyman. He stood clumsily, his cap in his hand.

"Weyman, you want me? What for?"

"I was coming about the doc, sir," said Weyman.

"What doctor?" snapped Gillespie.

"Doctor Kildare, sir. The boys call him *the* doc, because we've seen him around. We've seen him work."

"And what have you seen the *other* doctors doing? Never mind, never mind. What's this about Kildare?"

"The redhead, sir."

"Redhead—Kildare—the girl I was talking about? You discovered her, did you?"

"She's a bad lot. Her brother Nick is wanted for the killing of Bowler Smith."

"What killing?"

"A fellow called Bowler Smith that was talked about once with this redhead, this Rosalie. People heard Nick talking pretty mean and threatening about Smith. Nick followed him out of a joint the other evening into the street. There was a couple of cracks of a gun. People run out. Smith's lying dead. There's a trail of blood they follow a ways but the kid is gone. And he's Rosalie's brother."

"And Kildare is out of his head about that girl?"

"He's sunk."

Gillespie, breaking into a sudden roar, exclaimed: "Why do you trail the dirty gossip of the district into my office? I'm not Kildare's godfather. Off with you!"

Weyman disappeared.

Gillespie, alone, bowed his head and shrank smaller in his chair. He struck the arm of the chair as though he cursed that symbol of his age and his weakness. A fierce impatience came over him so that he thrust himself suddenly to his feet and went with a tottering step to a closet in the corner of the room. There he opened the door, picked out an overcoat, and huddled his arms into it. He took a hat from a shelf and jammed this on his head, but when he turned from the outer door of his office his strength which his savage burst of temper had given deserted him entirely.

He made only a single step before his legs gave way and he fell heavily forward on his face. Almost at once a knock came at his door. The sound of it made him twist desperately on the floor. He looked over his shoulder like a man in fear when the knock was repeated.

The fear in itself gave him an added strength which permitted him to sit up and grasp the arm of the wheel-chair, but when he attempted to rise he slipped and the weight of his falling body knocked the chair headlong away from him to the farther corner of the room.

With set teeth he crawled after it, one leg trailing hopelessly out behind him; and again the knock at the door, louder and far more prolonged, acted like a whip to urge him on. This time he managed to drag himself into the seat.

He hardly was settled there before the door opened. The frightened face of his office nurse looked in.

"Doctor, I thought I heard a fall ..."

"You did! You did!" shouted Gillespie. "You heard the fall of common sense around here. You heard it fall crash on its face. Why are you sticking your nose in here when you're not wanted? Can't a man shut his eyes for a moment of sleep without having his door battered down?"

"I'm sorry, doctor," said the nurse, but greater than her fear was the curiosity with which she stared at the hat crushed askew on the head of the diagnostician and the overcoat which he was wearing.

Glancing down at the coat, he realised her meaning.

"Common sense ought to make the hospital keep the place warmer!" he roared. "I have to put on street clothes to keep myself from pneumonia. Get out!"

"Yes, doctor!" said the nurse, and withdrew in soft-footed haste.

XIV

THREE MEN AND A GIRL

It was only a little after this that Mike the bartender, coming up the sidewalk towards his saloon, stepped into Kildare's dispensary and found it empty of patients.

"They giving you a breathing spell?" Mike asked, grinning. "Come in and have a beer with me?"

"Can't, Mike."

"What do you mean? Do what a man tells you to do and don't be arguing with your elders. Come along, doc. I've just broached a new keg and I've got to draw me a gallon of head to get me the pouring of a glass, there's that much life in it."

Kildare turned towards Mary Lamont. "If anyone comes in, I'll tap on the door of the saloon, doctor," she said.

So Kildare went with Mike.

"Do you mind that the boys are saying the doc is out of his wits and all in a dither about that pretty little red-head?" asked Mike, beaming over the beer.

"Redhead?" said Kildare. "I don't know any pretty little redheads."

Mike stared, aghast. The doc was lying to him. Mike now filled himself a good hooker of whisky and tossed it down. He gasped for air, swallowed, and blinked before he could speak.

"There wouldn't be a *one* redhead? There wouldn't be a Rosalie?"

"Rosalie?" said Kildare, his expression changing at once. "What about her?"

His stern voice shocked the bartender. "No harm meant," he protested. "I just noticed a pretty redhead."

"But her hair isn't red," answered Kildare.

"Her hair isn't what? What would it be if not red?"

"If you look closely at it in the light you'll see that it's a fine deep gold."

"Aye, very deep, very deep," said Mike. "But I've known Rosalie as a child, a growing brat, a young thing all legs and elbows and now whatever she is, and red is what I've always called her hair."

"Have you?" asked Kildare, surprised, smiling. "Well, Mike, there are a great many things to which we give names and never think of changing the labels although the facts become different enough."

"Now, what would you be meaning by that, at all?" asked Mike.

Kildare, lifting his head, still continued his smiling and what he saw with his inward eye was not the red face of Mike, be sure. "I mean there are ugly ducklings that turn into swans," he said.

"Oh, that's your meaning, is it? And let me tell you that there are dirty little ducks dressed up in swan's feathers, too!"

Kildare did not seem to hear. "Have you known Rosalie, always?"

"She's always been easy to know, if you foller me."

"It's true," said Kildare. "Only to hear her speak once tells a man what she is."

"Yes, sir, a word or two from Rosalie, and the boys know what she's all about," said Mike. After this broad stroke he waited, narrowing his eyes to see his words take effect.

Kildare merely nodded his head. His smiling never ceased and his gaze could not leave that bright tomorrow on which it was fixed.

"I understand," he said.

"Ah, but *do* you understand?" asked Mike.

"Of course I do," said Kildare. "There's a sort of beauty so warm and so real and so human that we take it all in at one grasp of the eye; it gives us a happiness that overflows, until we start laughing. I understand. I've looked at Rosalie and felt that way."

"Have you?" asked Mike, gloomily, drawing his brows down over his eyes.

"But tell me about her when she was a youngster," said Kildare.

"There was no hell raised in the Kitchen that she wasn't at the bottom of it," declared Mike.

"It's a wonder to me," said Kildare, unheeding, "that people in the Kitchen can carry on with everyday living when there's something like Rosalie to see and talk about."

"They've used her enough in their talk. Would you like to hear what they say?"

"Tell me, Mike. Yes, I want to hear that."

"They say," declared Mike, speaking with a slowness that gave emphasis, "that she's a loose thing altogether."

"Of course she is," answered Kildare. "She's as carefree as the wind that blows. Tell me more about her."

"I'm trying to tell you," said Mike, desperately, "but there's nothing I say that you'll understand."

Here there was a sharp rap at the side door which communicated with the dispensary, and Kildare, finishing his beer, turned away.

Mike watched him go in a sort of despair, his lips moving as he struggled to find speech. At last he shouted: "Doc!"

"Yes, Mike?" asked the doctor, turning back.

"I've got to tell you about her in one word!" cried Mike.

"Can you tell about Rosalie in a single word? Then you're a great poet, Mike!" laughed Kildare.

"This is the word, she—she—she's not what you think!"

"Is that what you're telling me?" asked Kildare, still laughing. "But I know she's not. I know that she's finer and higher than any thought of her."

And he went on into the dispensary. Mike, stunned, for a moment regarded empty space, then made a gesture of despair and reached for the whisky bottle as Weyman came striding in.

"Gimme a double shot," said Weyman. "Gillespie, the sour old swine, he won't do nothing to change the mind of the doc."

"Nobody could change his mind," declared Mike, heavily. "I dunno. Maybe he ain't got a mind left in him. I had him in here and told him all the facts as plain as the red nose on your dirty face, and he turned stinkweed into garden flowers right under my eyes."

At seven o'clock that evening, after the dispensary had been closed, Kildare turned in from the street under the porch of the vacant house and heard a quick, gasping voice say, sharply: "Who's that?"

"Hello, Red!" said Kildare. "Didn't you know me?"

"Sure, but I was kind of half expecting somebody else," said Red. "That mug of a plainclothes dick that sings in Mike's quartet—that Detective Flaherty—I seen him hanging around a couple of times today, and I kind of half thought—anyway, it's only you, doc!"

He sighed with the greatness of his relief.

"You mean that you think this Flaherty may suspect something?"

"Yeah. He always suspects things. He never expects anything good. It wouldn't pay him to."

"Is Rosalie down there with Nick?"

"Her? No, she's been and gone."

"Come—and gone again?" repeated Kildare, surprised. "Are you going down with me?"

"No. I'll stick around out here and watch. I dunno why I got Flaherty on my mind so much."

Kildare went down into the cellar, parting the darkness before him with the ray of the electric flashlight. He found Nick reading by lantern light and smoking. He had improved wonderfully in the last days. He put the magazine

133

down and said: "I always know your step, doc. Kind of quick and soft like you were overdue someplace and didn't want to wake anybody up as you came."

"You're a lot better."

"The only reason that I stick here is because you tell me to."

Kildare changed the bandage and looked at the wound.

"When you're on your feet," he said, "are you going to meet the law face to face, or are you going to slip away somewhere?"

"What chance would I have facing it?" demanded Nick. "They hear me damning Bowler Smith to his face and they know that I've got reason for hating him. Then they hear guns; they go out and find Bowler lying dead; and somebody sees me cutting away from the spot. That'd burn anybody, testimony like that. It's almost as good as eyewitnesses having seen the shooting."

"Why did you hate Bowler Smith?"

"Account of him passing some cracks about Rosalie."

"What sort of remarks, Nick?"

"Oh, I dunno. He was a dirty mug, that Bowler. He wasn't any loss to anybody." Nick had been annoyed by the question, obviously.

"What actually happened?" asked Kildare.

"You mean you don't know, and Rosalie didn't tell you? You mean you been doing all this for me not knowing whether I was a right guy or a rat?"

"I knew you were a right guy," said Kildare.

Nick, looking up at the doctor, flushed. "Here's the gospel about it. I see Bowler. I tick him off and tell him to

134

keep his mouth shut or I'll do him in. He leaves Joe Addison's place and I remember something I might've said to him and had forgotten. So I get up and go after him. It's just between twilight and night, you know? When the dark is almost there but the street lamps don't seem to take a good hold on it."

"I know," said Kildare.

"Anyway, I went out and called to Bowler and he turned. Just as he turned a fellow came up behind me from around the corner. He shoots right past my shoulder and the Bowler falls on his face. As I jump around, pulling my gun, I catch the second bullet right here, and it would have cooked me, all right, if it hadn't had to drill all the way through that gunmetal cigarette-case.

"I flop. It was like I'd been kicked in the chest and hit behind the head all at the same time. When I get my brains back, there's people around on the street and I see what's happened and how bad it looks for me. So I crawl away and get here; only Red spots me on the way but he's too good a kid to do anything but help. . . . When I get on my feet, I'm going to send Red to school. I'm going to send him through college from soup to nuts."

"A good idea," agreed Kildare. He looked at his watch.

"Are you believing what I've told you?" cried Nick, suddenly in an agony of suspense.

"Every word," answered Kildare. "I thought Rosalie would be here."

"She's upset about something. She came and went," said Nick.

"What's upset her?" asked Kildare.

135

"I dunno. When something really gripes her, she never lets on what the trouble is."

"Where would she be?"

"Why, at her place, I suppose."

"If she comes in while I'm out, tell her that I've gone there."

"Okay. And this is the last time I see you here."

"The last time?"

"If you keep coming, the cops will spot you one day and that'll put you in the soup."

"You're worth the chance, Nick."

"No, I'm not. But I'm going to be."

"So long, Nick."

"Promise me you're not coming again!"

"We'll see about that," said Kildare.

He went out into the night again, worried. The air was cold and clear with the tingle of frost in it. He put back his head and walked into that crispness feeling that he was facing towards happiness, if only he could keep himself from looking over his shoulder at all the hopes that lay dead behind him.

He had taken Rosalie home once so he knew her address though he never had been in her rooms. She was on the second floor of a walkup. He rang her bell once without response but when he tried the second time the latch of the front door clicked and he went up. He reached her door. It opened a crack and a voice hardly recognisable as Rosalie's asked who was there.

"It's I," said Kildare.

He waited, smiling, his hand on the knob. After a

moment, she said: "I can't see you, Jimmy. . . . I'm sorry. I can't."

He pushed the door open and stepped into a half-lighted hallway. There was no welcome from the girl. She stood back from him silently. She looked white; she had the tension of someone in pain.

"You're in trouble of some sort," said Kildare. "What is it?"

She shook her head quickly, without speaking.

"But wasn't this the evening of the big steak dinner?" he asked.

"Are you laughing at me?" she asked. "Are you laughing at me and despising me?"

"Come in here where I can look at you," said Kildare.

"I don't want to go into the light," she protested. "I'm not dressed, Jimmy."

The tousling of her hair made her head seem too big and in that light her features blurred like a picture out of focus. The sense of change in her sickened him a little.

In spite of that he put his arm around her and drew her towards the light into the nearest room. On the wall were a couple of signed photographs of actors; there were pictures of Rosalie, too, smiling as she looked up, smiling as she looked down, smiling as she looked over a bare shoulder. One of the pictures was what could only be called an art-study. He would not glance at it twice because he did not think that art had any right to go so far.

The whole room glowed with pink ruffles and chintz and lamps with rosy shades; Rosalie's favourite perfume was in the air everywhere; and somehow the scent of it was not so attractive as it always had been before.

He hardly could look at Rosalie herself, she was so pale. To see her without make-up was like watching a sunrise without colour. The effect was rather wintry. She wore a loose dressing-gown. He looked not away from her but slightly above her, preferring his expectation and his dream to the actuality.

She kept standing away from him in a manner that made him feel more of a handless gawk than he had been since childhood.

"Jimmy, what's been said to you about me today?" she asked. "Why don't you tell me?"

"But nothing's been said about you today," answered Kildare. "Nothing except Nick telling me that you didn't seem very well; oh, yes, and there was Mike."

"Ah—Mike!" she whispered.

"He loves you," said Kildare.

"Mike? Loves me?" repeated Rosalie, a strange smile flashing on her face and going out instantly.

"Of course he does. He said that he'd known you ever since you were a child and he wanted to tell me about you."

"Did he?" asked the girl.

"As a matter of fact, I should have listened more to Mike. But I started to do some talking about you. I couldn't help it."

A glimmer of light was beginning to come up in her eyes, but still she watched him with a hungry breathlessness, her glance running back and forth across his face.

138

"So in the end I'm afraid that I did all the talking about you," said Kildare. "Mike gave up trying."

"Ah, Jimmy!" said the girl.

"Now, what's the matter, really?" he asked. "Headache? I'm a doctor, you know, after all."

"Jimmy, Jimmy, God bless you!" said the girl.

She started towards him and he met her half-way. She seemed strangely small in slippers without heels, but just as he put his arms around her she made herself taller again by rising on her toes. The wintry sense of age was gone; happiness lifted her as wings lift a bird.

"I want you to consider something," said Kildare. "I haven't a bean in the world. . . ."

"Money's rotten. All money's rotten, rotten, rotten; and all the people who get it are rotten, too."

"Besides, I'm in such a bad way over at the hospital that I don't even know that they'll let me finish my intern year there."

"That old hospital is a fool!"

"But in spite of all that I'm not, I'm asking you if you'd consider marrying me some day, Rosalie?"

"Yes, yes!" Then before the joy had penetrated him she was saying: "No, they wouldn't let me!"

"Who wouldn't let you?"

"Oh, the whole world would be against it!"

"Damn the world," said Kildare. "It's already damned, for that matter, so why should we have to care about it?"

He drew back a little and saw that her eyes were closed. To prevent them more securely from looking into the future, she had placed one hand across them.

139

"So you're going to marry me, Rosalie, aren't you?"

"Do you love me, Jimmy?"

"My dear, what have I been saying to you just now?"

"But let's not talk about marriage for a minute. You know, Jimmy, marriage can be a horrible thing. The legal chains begin to rattle, after a while."

"What in the world are you talking about?" asked Kildare.

"Nothing—nothing—" she said. "Nothing at all, if you don't want to hear it."

XV

HOMECOMING

When Kildare got back to the hospital at midnight, he found a telegram waiting in his room from his father. It said:

> I NEED YOU VERY BADLY, HOPE
> YOU CAN COME OUT AT ONCE.

He tried to make the uttermost meaning out of the few words. If it had been something that concerned his mother his father would have used "we". But the old doctor spoke only of himself, and this troubled Kildare a little less.

His next task was to get permission to leave the hospital at once. Carew's office, of course, had been closed for six or seven hours, and there remained in the place only one authority sufficient to give him leave of absence.

So he went to Gillespie.

The waiting-room of the great man was empty. The nurse on duty stole into the inner office which the internist used as a bedroom also and came out to report that Gillespie was not asleep; he would see Kildare.

The diagnostician lay like "my son John, one shoe off

and one shoe on", partly undressed, an old-fashioned flannel nightgown huddled on him awry. Kildare knew, without asking, the constant agony which kept the old man from sleep. He was reading a book and said, without looking up: "Here's a fellow that hasn't much use for certain types of women. He says: 'Young men choose their women by candlelight, and find they are angels to woo and devils when won. He buys her for a high price and finds that he has sold himself. As long as credulity pays, it is easy for her to believe. She takes the name of virtue if she is afraid of change, but she will trust herself to the discreet thief.' Rather an indictment, Kildare, eh?"

Kildare said: "I wonder if it isn't always easy to seem wise at the expense of something beautiful and great."

"Perhaps, perhaps," Gillespie snarled. "But what do you want with me now?"

"You remember my father, sir?"

"Father? Have you got a father?"

"You saw him once in the hospital not many weeks ago, sir."

"Did I? Bicarbonate of soda—yes, I remember. What about him?"

"I have a telegram from him saying that he needs me."

"Probably an exaggeration. Why should anybody need a young intern who is not even a doctor? Or *are* you a doctor, Kildare?"

"Not until my intern year is finished, sir."

"And are you going to finish it?"

142

"I hope so, sir."

"Carew tells me there's a doubt of that. He has his eye on you, Kildare, and I'm forced to say that he's not pleased. Of course all this means nothing to me."

"No, sir," said Kildare.

"Don't answer me like a wooden-headed English butler. The fact is that you're close to losing your place. Do you know what that means?"

"It means the end of me as a doctor."

"What's the hospital to do, I ask you, with interns who go about giving blood transfusions to unknown patients?"

"Who reports that I've done that?"

"You were going to give one, weren't you?"

"I was unable to get the blood and the instruments from the hospital, sir."

"I don't care what you were not able to get. You gave the transfusion, didn't you?"

Kildare was silent.

"Answer me!" shouted Gillespie.

"Yes, sir," said Kildare.

"Who did you give it to?"

Kildare said nothing.

"Who bribed you?" demanded Gillespie.

The silence of Kildare continued.

Gillespie hitched himself up on one elbow and shook a forefinger at him, saying: "What was your price?"

"I don't take money, doctor," said Kildare.

"There are other bribes than money. Danger itself is

enough of a bribe to get young idiots into trouble, to say nothing of the praise of half-wits or the smiling of some wench!"

"I came to see you," said Kildare, calmly diverging from the subject, "in order to ask your permission to have a day or two of leave from the hospital. . . ."

"Are you answering my question, or are you not? Are you throwing away your whole career for some thug or some shoddy little light of love?"

"I came to ask for a few days of leave," said Kildare.

"I've put the question to you that has to be answered!" said Gillespie.

"I take it," said Kildare, "that I shall not have the time off."

Gillespie sank back on the couch. "Take all the leave you want. You have my leave to go. You have my leave never to come back. Do exactly as you please," he said.

As he lay back, he dropped the book on his chest so that the title came clearly under the eyes of Kildare, and he was able to see, printed large across the back: *The Ductless Glands*, by Liddell and Hartman.

So certainly it was not from the book but from his own brain that Gillespie had produced certain bitter sayings about women. After a moment Kildare said: "I'm sorry, doctor."

"Who's that? Who's there?" asked Gillespie, opening his closed eyes. "Is that you, Kildare? What do you want, my boy?"

"Nothing, sir," said Kildare, and went suddenly from the room.

He telephoned to his home in Dartford and his father's voice answered at once.

"The telegram you sent at six did not catch me until just now," said Kildare. "I can catch the one o'clock and get out there by two-thirty. Is Mother all right?"

"Mother? She's fine."

"And you, Father?"

"It's not for us that I need you. But there's a case. . . ."

"I'll be out on the one o'clock. Don't meet the train. I'll take the taxi home."

The one o'clock picked up the late theatre crowd. Half the men sat asleep; the women only nodded, continuing to smile in the drowsing. Women are queer. For sins of omission and commission men always are forgiven unless the law catches up with them; but there is no forgiveness for women.

But then how many women are like Rosalie? She had been unhappy about something when he saw her that evening in her rooms; she had been pale and weary with hopelessness; but he had made her bloom before he left.

Beyond windows in the dark of the night, he was aware of a certain familiarity of silhouettes and knew they were coming into Dartford. When he got off the train, he saw the tall, gaunt figure of his father waiting. A pang struck through Kildare. The pain that was in him made him realise how greatly sorrow is compounded with all life,

145

and there was a certain tenderness in the greeting he gave the old man.

Perhaps it was this that made Stephen Kildare say: "Aren't you growing up too fast, Jimmy?"

"Growing old, you mean, don't you?" asked Kildare.

They kept looking gravely and kindly at one another for a moment and then they laughed a little.

"This will do you good," said Stephen Kildare, before they stepped into the old automobile. He waved his hand at the sheen of the night sky and obscure shadows of houses and trees which composed Dartford. "The air's different."

"And the people," said Kildare. "How different *they* are!"

He leaned far back in the seat, smiling and shaking his head.

"Out here," said Stephen Kildare, "men have time to stop and look at one another; in the city all they see is the next dollar. Maybe they get lots of dollars but they don't get lots of life."

"Are you making the wrong turn, here?"

"No. I'm running up the hill to drop in on old Galt. He's the case I want you to take a look at, Jimmy, to-morrow. Doesn't sleep much, and it comforts the old chap to have me look in on him whenever I can."

When they got to the Galt house his father said: "I'll just pop in and out again in a minute. Give him a chance to grouch a bit. That clears up his system and he goes to sleep with a smile. Age is a poisonous diet, Jimmy."

He was getting out with his bag as he spoke. Kildare got out too.

"I'll go in with you," he said.

"Why, I wouldn't do that," protested his father, surprised.

"But this is the case you want me to see, isn't it?"

"This case? Yes, yes, that's true. Of course. Well, but old Galt is a touchy devil, and he doesn't expect you."

"I don't mind touchy people," said Kildare, and smiled at the thought.

"Well, come along," said his father.

As they went up to the door Kildare slipped his hand through his father's arm.

"I'm afraid that you may have thought you were getting a rising young diagnostician out here, Father. The fact is that I should have written to you a few days ago. I'm only a common or garden intern, now. I couldn't do the work for Gillespie."

"Not—do—the work?" gasped Stephen Kildare.

"He needs a man; he found out that I was a boy. . . . That's all."

"That's a quote, isn't it?"

"Yes, those are his words."

"Didn't he know your age before he hired you?"

"He knew my age. But years are not what he's thinking of. It's the knowledge of life that makes a fellow a man first and a doctor afterwards. Those are more of his words. Are you terribly disappointed?"

"Not disappointed. Surprised," said Stephen Kildare,

speaking slowly. "What surprises me is that Gillespie should have been wrong about you in the first place. He's not the man to make mistakes like that. You may not please him, but I think that you still could please Dartford, Jimmy."

"No," said Kildare. "In all but words I've told my hometown that it was too small to fit me; now if I'm not good enough to suit the city, I'm not good enough to suit Dartford. That's always the way. If you go away from home, you've got to make good or be damned."

And his father, thoughtfully stretching out his hand to ring the doorbell, nodded his head in honest, silent agreement. As they waited for an answer, he laid a hand on his son's shoulder. They said nothing because they did not need to speak.

A maid with a tired, all-night face opened the door and managed a weary smile for the benefit of the doctor. "He's bad," she said. "I hear his bed creaking when he turns, and it ain't stopped creaking for hours."

"Ten years ago, tuberculosis," explained Stephen Kildare. "And from all clinical evidence I thought it had healed. But now I think there is a recurrence. It won't be easy considering his age.

"And he is a worrying man, Jimmy. He thinks that the bank can't get along without him, though Harry is a fine man and doing well with the banking business, everybody tells me.

"I suspected typhoid or malaria at first. It must be that tuberculosis process flaring up despite the lack of activity in the X-ray plates. The fibrosis in both lung fields remains the same; of course, renal or intestinal involvement but no other symptoms indicating it. This fever (temperature) swing has been going on for some time."

He paused at the landing in the stairway. Through the window they could hear the outbreak of a small commotion in the barn. A horse stamped and snorted; a goat bleated.

"Galt still believes in goat's milk?" asked Kildare smiling.

"Won't drink anything else," declared Stephen Kildare. "He imported some new goats from Texas only a few weeks ago. He says people that use goat's milk add ten years to their lives. If he adds ten to his, he'll have all the money in the world!"

"What have you been giving him?"

"The usual treatment. Rest, tonics, diet, Blaud's pills—anything to improve his resistance. . . . Well, here we are."

"It seems to me," said Kildare, "that you have the case pretty well in mind and in hand."

"Oh, I think so," nodded his father. He added quickly: "But I thought that old Galt is so important out here that I'd better get the best advice I could on him; and that's why my mind turned to you, Jimmy. You ought to have a lot of new-fangled ideas in your system, by this time."

Kildare was frowning a little as he entered the room behind Stephen Kildare. The feverish eyes of old John Galt turned towards them.

"Aren't you good enough by yourself, Kildare?" he

snapped. "Are you getting old? Do you have to get help?"

"This is only Jimmy," said the old doctor. "He just dropped in with me to say hello."

"Dartford wasn't big enough for him," said John Galt. "Why's he back here? Has he shrunk some while he was away? How are they using you, Jimmy?" he asked. "Don't mind me. Old men are all mean, and lying in bed, it sweats my meanness right up to the surface. My family can't stand me any more."

Kildare made no effort to examine the old man. He was more intent on a thought which had come to him when he heard a fresh commotion in the barn and again the bleating voice of a goat. When he was in the car with his father again, he said: "About two weeks of that low grade temperature?"

"Just about."

"They're a bad problem, sometimes," said Kildare.

"Even for you big fellows?" laughed his father. "What new things are you city chaps up to? Is the vaccine still the accepted treatment?"

"I haven't seen many of the cases in the city," said Kildare, "but there are reports of excellent results with sulphanilamide."

"Sulphanilamide? Sulphanilamide? That's the new cure-all, isn't it? That's the scatter-shot that's bound to hit something? You know, Jimmy, I go a little easy on those new ideas."

"Quite right, too," said Kildare. "But adequately controlled blood-work gives an index of the reaction of sulphanilamide. That's why it's safe. And in the case of Galt—that continued low grade temperature—he's really pretty badly off, just now, isn't he?"

"Jimmy," said his father, soberly, "I think it's nothing but faith in me that keeps him together, I'm worried about John Galt. He's old, but there's use in him still, and years of it, if I can get him past this. But it's my worry; I don't want to put a load on your shoulders. I wish I could get that fever down."

"It's rather like malaria or undulant fever, isn't it?" suggested Kildare.

"Undulant fever? There's none of that around here. Comes from goats and cows down South, mostly," said the old man.

Suddenly he braked the car almost to a stop. He snapped his bony fingers loudly.

"Those damned Texas goats!" he exclaimed.

"What did you say?" asked Kildare.

"Why, the goats he brought up here from Texas!"

"Oh—I didn't think of that," said the son, biting his lip a little and successfully keeping back the smile.

"Didn't you? You have to watch the small details, the background of a case, Jimmy, if you're going to pry into all the facts about a disease. Goats from Texas —and then this fever—I'm going to drop you at the house and run straight back for a blood specimen. But I'll need some of the bacterial antigen of brucella melitensis . . ."

151

"I can telephone to the hospital and have some here for you by special messenger in the morning."

"Good boy, Jimmy! You know, it turned out rather lucky, after all, that I asked you to come out here! This sulphanilamide—does it knock over brucella melitensis?"

"Symptom-free in twenty-four hours."

XVI

THOSE WHO WILL NOT SEE

He sat alone with his mother in the kitchen, drinking strong black coffee. "It's the only bad thing your father ever did in the world: he gave you the coffee habit," said Martha Kildare. "How do you think he's looking?"

Kildare smiled. "He? Oh, *he's* all right."

"You ought to be over there at the dance," said Martha Kildare. "It won't break up till four or five. It's for the benefit of the new fire engine. They're holding it in the Hall. Why don't you step over there, Jimmy?"

"I'll stay here till Father gets back," said Kildare. "And we can talk."

"There's a reason why you should look in on that dance," she said. "Beatrice is there."

"Beatrice doesn't worry much about me now," he said. "She knows that I'm more a doctor than a man."

When he thought of this, he smiled again. He felt that he was being a bit enigmatical and did not mind the effect. He added: "She wrote to me that I was to forget our engagement."

"Did she mean she wondered if you *wanted* to forget it?" asked his mother.

He made a queer, inclusive gesture, saying: "I've

153

asked a girl to marry me. I asked her today. It wasn't Beatrice." He waited. Then he said: "Why are there tears in your eyes?"

"I don't know. Perhaps it makes me feel a bit behind the times. Tell me about her, Jimmy. Have you her picture?"

"No, but imagine a girl with golden-red hair—and beautiful—and kind. She's terribly kind."

"Would I love her?"

"No. Not at once."

"Why wouldn't I?"

"I don't know. But you wouldn't. Not at once."

"Do you mean that she would need some explaining?"

"Perhaps. What I really mean is that she isn't your type."

"Would she have to be explained to your father?"

"I suppose she would. I wish I hadn't thought about that."

"We won't talk about her, if you don't wish."

"I ought to wish to talk about her, but not exactly here." He looked about the room, troubled by his own reactions.

"You've just come back, darling, and you feel a little strange with us."

"I feel a little queer, not strange."

"About me?"

"No, not about you."

"About your father?"

"How could I feel strange about Father?" he asked, rather sharply.

"You wonder why he called you out here?"

"It wasn't for John Galt. That's all I know," he said.

She put the back of her hand against her forehead. After a while he said: "Don't explain. Don't tell me anything that hurts. You don't have to. I love you too much to want that."

She said: "Doctor Gillespie told your father to ask you to come out here. He told us to hold you here for several days."

Kildare got up and took a step or two. "You heard from him in the afternoon?" he asked.

"Yes. He said that you weren't working with him any longer."

"That's true. I've told Father. For you, I wanted to wait till you had sunlight to hear it by. I'm a bust. I couldn't do the work."

"Jimmy, does it make you feel like a failure?"

"I'm not a failure. Not yet," he said. "I'm a good doctor. I know that. Things are as clear as A B C to me that are obscure to a good many others in my profession. I can be a *good* doctor but I want to be a *great* one. I'm ambitious, I mean; there's something in me that I want to grow up to. I wasn't good enough for Gillespie but still I'm going to be a diagnostician. There's nobody like him. Being with him was like being at the Wishing Gate; but if I can't have him, I'll start more slowly and try to get to the same end."

"I think he's a cruel man!"

He stood behind her chair and put his hand on her head. "Don't say that," said Kildare. "There's no cruelty in him. He's hard but he's just. He's about the greatest man," he added, slowly, "that I'll ever know."

"You always mean what you say," she said. "He's a great man; he's not cruel; and you're not good enough for him."

"It draws blood," said Kildare. "But I'll have to say that that's right. . . ." His voice died away. He began to smile faintly.

She waited. "About this girl, son," she began. "I'm a little worried about her. Yes. Yes, I am. I want you to do something to clear your eyes."

"Of course I'll do whatever you say," said Kildare. "But aren't you being a little bit mysterious?"

"Even mothers are a little mysterious to the Jimmy Kildares of this world," she said, with tears in her eyes again. "I want you to go over and see the dance for a while. Tell Beatrice that you're engaged to another girl and see if she's really glad."

"Should I do that?"

"I think you should."

"I suppose it's better if I do," murmured Kildare.

He went over through the dark of the night and saw the light outside the Dartford Hall widening out across the street like the blare of a bugle. The dance floor was one storey up. There was a coat-and-hat room to pass through first. A dozen of the lads of the town were in the anterooms smoking cigarettes, passing a flask around, and laughing, and looking askance at the world to make sure that it was aware of their devilry.

He paid a dollar for a ticket and went in through the cluster of idlers.

Twisted, coloured streamers flowed across the big room, below the rafters. A mist of random and illegal cigarette smoke rose towards the lights, which were much too dim. Around the wall the elders and the women sat. The men circulated. They all seemed very much at home. Now and then they cut antics.

Beatrice Raymond sat at one side with young Harry Galt. He went straight towards them. Harry was embarrassed. He said: "Hello, Jimmy. Beatrice thought that she'd like to take in this ..."

Kildare laughed. He sat down beside Beatrice on the other side. Harry Galt murmured an excuse about something and went away.

"What's the matter?" asked Kildare. "He acts as though I owned you."

"He's used to the idea, even if it was a sort of absentee landlordship," said Beatrice.

"Are you feeling sour about me?"

"No, why should I?" she asked.

"Because we were engaged," said Kildare, "and then I went away and didn't write, like a pig. I know now what you must have felt for a while."

"Do you really know?" she asked.

"I really know," he nodded.

"Then you're in love—at last?" she asked.

She wore a dress of rose colour with a flaring skirt. She kept looking down and flaring the skirt a bit and smiling as though at a secret knowledge.

He was worried by this but he said: "Yes. I've asked a girl to marry me."

157

Beatrice kept on flaring the skirt, making the folds of it lighter by tossing them up in the air a little.

"Don't be a pig, Beatrice," said Kildare.

She was silent.

"I mean, you're not going to be mysterious and silent about it, are you? We're always pals, Skinny, aren't we?"

She still kept looking down and nodded. She said nothing.

"I'm getting nervous," said Kildare. "Say something, Skinny, will you?"

She turned her head sharply, looking away down the hall.

"I'm not so skinny any more, am I?" she asked.

"Maybe you're not," said Kildare. "But be nice, Skinny, will you?"

"I'll be anything I can, for you," said Beatrice.

"Shall we dance or something?"

"No, thanks. I have this dance with Harry. Here we are, Harry! This is ours, isn't it?"

She stood up and danced away with Harry Galt, who looked a little astonished. And as she turned, he saw her smiling. It seemed rather a fixed smile, though her eyes were extraordinarily bright; they were as bright as tears, even.

He went home, tiptoed into the kitchen and found his mother still there at her sewing. She put a finger on her lips and smiled at him and pointed.

"In bed?" he asked, smiling back.

"In bed, and sound. Are you through with the dance so soon? And you saw Beatrice?"

158

"I saw her."

"And what did she say?"

"Oh, she didn't care."

"She didn't what!" exclaimed Mrs. Kildare.

"My dear old dear," said Kildare, laughing a little, "you mustn't think that a lovely girl like Beatrice would care very much about a downyheaded fellow like me. She needs something brighter; she deserves it; I hope she has it, too!"

"Is that the way you feel?"

"Yes, and yet there's a sort of sense of loss. As though a pound had been cut away from close to the heart. You know what I mean?"

"I hope I know," said Martha Kildare. "And Beatrice didn't care?"

"No, not a bit. I think Harry Galt means something, now. As a matter of fact, after I told her, she hardly looked at me."

"Did she keep her head down?" asked Martha Kildare.

"How did you guess that, Mother?" asked Kildare.

"Oh, I don't know. Perhaps it's because I'm a woman myself. Didn't she meet your eye at all?"

"No, not once. I thought that was rather queer."

"It wasn't like Beatrice, was it?"

"No, it really wasn't. I always knew her as well—as well . . ."

"As well as you ever knew a man?"

"That's exactly it. Like a man, but better, somehow!" He yawned.

"I think you're sleepy, Jimmy."

159

"Yes. I'll turn in, if you don't mind."

"You'd better. And—how long it is since you've said your prayers?"

"Why, let me see—a thousand years, almost."

"You'd better say a few tonight."

"Should I?"

"Yes, perhaps. Ask God to forgive you, my dear."

"All right. But for what?"

"Oh, for things in general," she said. "We all need forgiveness now and then, don't we?"

XVII

ONE STEP NEARER

The special messenger from the hospital arrived with the bacterial antigen early in the morning. The test proved that John Galt had undulant fever and an injection of sulphanilamide was given at once. Kildare waited until the temperature began to fall; then he took a train back to New York. He went not to the hospital but straight to the vacant house where Nick was lying.

It was one of those miserable days when the rain was alternating with sleet and freezing on the pavements where it fell.

Kildare, getting out of the taxi one block from the house, skidded half a dozen times before he turned in under the high porch and opened the cellar door. It would be his last visit.

A light shone from the half-open door of Nick's hideout, glimmering through a thin cloud of cigarette smoke. Nick was sitting up with a couple of pillows behind his shoulders while Red was reading aloud from a magazine, tracing out the words with the tip of his grubby finger.

"Break it up, Red," said Nick. "Hi, doc. It's a long time. But it's not long enough. You promised that you wouldn't come back here again."

161

"I didn't promise," answered Kildare. He studied the brighter eye and the improved colour of his patient and smiled. "You're as tough as india-rubber, Nick," he said.

"Sure, I'm all right. Barge along out of this. Will you?"

"I'll go pretty soon. It's my last trip down here and I want to make sure that you're all right," said Kildare.

"I'll go keep an eye peeled," suggested Red.

"Sit still, Red," said Kildare. "The three of us may not be together again for a long time. How's Rosalie?"

"On her toes like I never saw her before. You ask her a plain question and she just laughs, kind of foolish and happy. She's got more bubble in her than ginger ale," said Red.

Kildare, on one knee as he took Nick's pulse, said quietly: "I hope I can keep her as happy as that all her life."

"You hope what?" asked Nick, startled.

"We're going to be married," answered Kildare.

"Married?" breathed Nick. Colour burned into his face. "Like hell you are!" he said.

"Are you dead against it? What's the matter, Nick?"

"She can't do that to you," declared Nick.

"Steady, Nick. I'm not good enough for her, but after all if she wants . . ."

"She wants the world with a fence around it. Sure she does. But she's not going to get it," Nick broke in, his face still dark with blood.

Out in the corridor a foot crashed loudly against one of the scattered boxes that were ranged along the wall. Red jumped for the doorway. As he reached it a strong

162

light flashed into his face and he sprang back again, crying over his shoulder with almost soundless lips, "It's Flaherty!"

"Then—God help him!" said Nick through his teeth, and dragged his gun from beneath the bedding.

"Give me that," commanded Kildare.

"Back up, you fool!" said Nick under his breath. "He's going to put the rap on you, doc!"

Kildare grabbed the gun and pulled it from Nick's hand as Flaherty said from the doorway: "How's everybody and everything? Sorry to see you in here, doc."

A powerful electric flash streamed through the doorway. Kildare could make out the revolver which was pointing towards him.

"Okay, doc," said Flaherty. "I'll take the rod you're holding there."

Kildare walked forward into the light. "You'll have no trouble with me."

"I didn't think so. My name's Flaherty."

"Detective Flaherty? I'm glad to know you. I've heard Mike talk about you." Kildare passed over the gun.

"The way he'll slap my ears down for this will be nobody's business," said Flaherty. "I wish to God it had been anybody else in the world than you, doc. Well, I had a kind of a happy home, there in Sullivan's saloon for twenty years, but I'll be in the dog-house now!"

He had put up his gun as he spoke. A moment later a small form flew past Kildare and caught the legs of Flaherty with a football tackle.

"Smack him now, doc! Smack him!" screamed Red.

Kildare loosed Red's grip and straightened him up.

"We're not smacking anybody," he said. "I'm sorry, Flaherty."

"So am I," said Flaherty. "I wish to God that I'd never been dragged into this. But seeing the kid sneak down in here a couple of times I had to come and investigate. And here we are!"

Nick made a helpless gesture with both hands. "I knew it that first night," he said. "I knew that I'd pull you down in the gutter along with me. I wish . . ."

"Stop that!" said Kildare, sharply. "I don't regret what I've done."

"They'll smash you just as sure as they'll burn me," said Nick. "I told Rosalie to keep you away from here. I told Rosalie that you were doing fine."

"Why don't you shut up, kid?" asked Flaherty. "You might be naming a lot of names that I'd have to listen to."

"You understand, Nick?" said Kildare. "You owe me nothing. I'm proud of what I've done for you, and I know you're honest."

"Shut up that crying, Red, will you?" asked Flaherty.

"I wasn't making no noise," sobbed Red.

Flaherty said: "Doc, I guess I don't need to book you just yet. I can pick you up when I want you, can't I?"

"Certainly," said Kildare. "It's kind of you, Flaherty."

"Mike and Weyman are gunna tell me how kind I've been," said Flaherty sadly. "This kid Nick I oughta take down to the police hospital. But maybe he's too sick to stand that long haul. Maybe, it'd be better to take him over to your place, doc?"

He winked as he spoke and Kildare managed to smile.

Ten minutes later he was in the hospital. He went up to his room and washed and shaved; before he had finished the loud-speaker was summoning him to Carew.

The rumour had gone like quicksilver through the hospital. When he stepped into the corridor he met Tom Collins coming on the run. Collins, panting, took him by the arm and walked down the hall with him towards the elevator. He said nothing until they reached the elevator.

"It was one of those things that had to be done, was it?" asked Collins.

"I thought so," said Kildare.

"I've seen the kid," said Collins. "They've got him up in the surgical ward."

Even the elevator man knew what had happened. He looked at Kildare with eyes of wonder, of admiration, and of respect. "Sorry, doc," he muttered when he let Kildare out on the top floor.

Down the hall a pair of chattering nurses stopped their talk and looked at him with big eyes as he went by. The whole world had put on a funereal aspect; and this was almost as definitely the end of him as though he were to be put under ground. The full sense of the thing would not come home to him but he knew that the bitterness and the despair would come later on when he found himself with empty hands in a world of infinite vacancy.

Then he was standing before Carew.

Carew said: "Some men are born for trouble. I think this is the fourth or fifth time you've been before me, Doctor Kildare; the majority of my interns never stand once on this carpet."

Kildare waited, silently. There was after all nothing this man could do except to give definitely the blow which he already expected and was prepared for.

"It is said," went on Carew, "that you have given assistance to a known criminal without reporting the case. I cannot ask you to incriminate yourself...."

"It's true," said Kildare.

The door of the office pushed open as Carew was saying, "You make a free confession?"

"Of course he would," said the voice of Gillespie, as he wheeled himself in. "Every young jackass has to bray. How long are you going to spend pulling his teeth, Carew? I want to talk to you about the Clifford case."

"Until the law makes the definite charge," said Carew, "there is nothing for me to do except to prepare Doctor Kildare for what inevitably must come: his dismissal from this hospital."

"What makes you so sure of everything, Walter?" asked Gillespie. "Suppose he were to turn up evidence that this lad Nick is not a criminal after all, but simply a victim? That'd change the attitude of the law, wouldn't it?

"But you're right, after all. Some men, when they're in a corner, put their heads down and fight their way out. But a fellow like Kildare throws up his hands and lets the course of events walk right over his face. If the law wants a victim, he'll be the scapegoat. Get rid of him, now. I have to talk to you."

That was how Kildare found himself again in the corridor, one long step nearer to the end. He started for the surgical ward and Nick.

XVIII

TAKE YOUR HEART OFF YOUR SLEEVE

At Nick's bedside a big, uniformed policeman instantly moved up within earshot.

Nick said, happily: "You still on the loose? That means they'll never hang the rap on you—and am I glad of that!" He added to the policeman: "Lookit, big boy. This is Doc Kildare. You know what he is to me. Are you gunna horn in on this, or stick some cotton in your ears?"

"I gotta listen to every word," said the policeman, looking curiously at Kildare. "But maybe today I can hear better from a long ways off."

He sauntered down the aisle towards the farther end of the ward and Nick said: "They been and examined me. A big shot. A police lieutenant. He said he hoped I had a chance of beating the rap and the chair. You think I have, doc?"

"Of course you have," lied Kildare. "But I want to go back to something in your case, Nick. What started you after Smith was something he'd said about Rosalie?"

"That was it."

"Did you hear him say it?"

"No."

"Who told you about it?"

"The best friend I've got, next to you."

"What's the name of that best friend?"

"Happy Leeman. He's a good guy if there ever was one. He puts something in everybody's drink."

"Where could I find him?"

"Why, he's got a room over Thompson's butcher shop. But what d'you want out of him, doc?"

"Something better than fun," said Kildare.

He went out of the hospital to find Happy Leeman but his hope of success was very small—even if he located the man.

Kildare went slowly up the street and turned in towards Sullivan's saloon. Before him, he saw Weyman, striding big, slam through the door, and as Kildare entered he heard the great voice of the ambulance driver shouting, "Where's that crumb Flaherty?"

An avenue opened magically through the crowd and exposed the unhappy figure of Flaherty next to the bar. Mike, folding his arms, said loudly: "Yeah, I guess you come over to congratulate Flaherty, didn't you? I been telling him how proud I am of him, too. The whole district is proud of him. He's done a fine thing, he has."

Flaherty called out: "Keep off from me, Weyman. If you try to put them big hams of yours on me, I'll drill you as sure as hell. I'm on duty, you dummy. I'm an officer of the law, you fool. Weyman, back up, will you?"

But Weyman, taking long and steady strides, showed not the least intention of backing up. That was why Kildare said, sharply: "Wait a minute, Weyman!"

The whole saloon had been a-buzz with voices until

he spoke; and now silence like a visible wave washed across the room. Their eyes followed Kildare as he walked in between Weyman and Flaherty and led them both to the bar.

"I'm buying this drink," he said. "Weyman is a partner of mine, Flaherty, and Flaherty is as good a fellow as the law allows him to be. I want you in on this, Mike. We're drinking all around. Good luck to the lot of us!"

The beer glass raised automatically in Weyman's hand, but it seemed almost to strangle him before it would go down. He rested an elbow on the bar and shook his head. "Why did you do it, Flaherty?"

Kildare answered for Flaherty. "It was his job and he had to do it. But we don't want the quartet broken up by a thing like that, do we?"

"Look!" said Mike, deeply moved. "He's talkin' for *you*, Flaherty, you rat!"

Flaherty could not speak. He could only drink.

"Do you know a fellow called Happy Leeman?" Kildare asked Weyman.

"Yeah, why?"

"He may be a little less happy than usual when I'm through with him," said Kildare, and left the saloon. Weyman, calling loudly behind him, started in pursuit, but Kildare went heedlessly on. He crossed the street, turned down a block, and then climbed the stairs to the lodgings above Thompson's butcher shop. To his first rap a cheerful voice called out an invitation to enter, and so he walked into the home of Happy Leeman.

· · · · ·

It was just about then that Rosalie was shown, without a pause in the waiting-room, straight into the office of Gillespie.

"This is mighty kind of you," said Gillespie, "to come here just because I've asked you. I'm glad to see you for a couple of reasons."

"Are you, doctor—really?" she asked.

"Of course I'm glad," said Gillespie. "In the first place, there's that hat you've got on. I have a grand-niece who's having a birthday before long, and if I could find the sister of that hat you're wearing, it would improve that girl a whole lot. But I'm not a rich man, so I'll ask how much that hat cost, if you don't mind?"

"It was twenty-three seventy-five," said Rosalie, "but it was marked down from thirty-five."

"Thirty-five dollars for something that would hardly cover my fist?" Gillespie smiled. "Now, how would you account for all that cost? It is maybe the feather?"

"No," said Rosalie, "it's not the feather, but the angle it's stuck into the hat."

"I've heard of people paying a lot of money for political angles," said Gillespie, "but I've never heard of them paying for feather angles on hats. Thirty-five dollars, eh?"

"It's robbery, isn't it?" said Rosalie, beginning to relax. "But that's the Paris of it, you know."

"I suppose it is," agreed Gillespie, "but I wonder how much Paris a young intern could pay for?"

She lifted her head suddenly, alarmed and on guard. Then she said, with dangerous brightness in her eyes and that same sharp directness: "I think you're talking about Doctor Kildare."

"He *is* a little far from Paris just now, isn't he?" asked Gillespie.

"What do you want me to do?"

"About Jimmy?"

"Yes."

"Help to make him happy. That's all any of us can do for one another."

"That's what I want for him. His happiness."

"Good," said Gillespie. "We're going to get on beautifully. Kildare has plenty of friends, and a mother and father, but perhaps you and I are the ones most interested in his happiness. What do you think?"

"You?" she cried. "But you've tortured him!"

She was afraid that she had gone too far in that outbreak, and she caught up a hand to her face.

"Perhaps I have," agreed Gillespie. "I've hammered him to try to get him in shape, and perhaps I'll hammer him again. But in a vague way he understands what I'm after. Or does he begin to hate me?"

She considered a moment, anxiously, before she decided on the truth. "No," she said, "because you understand how he is."

"Not exactly."

She explained: "He doesn't damn his enemies, even. He keeps turning the cheek so fast that it makes my head swim. And you? No, he doesn't hate you, Doctor Gillespie." She cried out, "What do you want me to do?"

"Just what I said before. I want you to give Kildare as much happiness as possible."

"No," she said huskily. "I think you want to take him away from me."

"Why should I?" asked Gillespie. "And *how* could I, which is more to the point."

She fought against making the admission, her eyes almost closed by pain. At last she said: "He thinks that you're the greatest man in the world."

The compliment he brushed aside as of no value, merely saying: "Then it seems that I have a hold on him; so have you. But first tell me how you would go about assuring the happiness of our friend Kildare."

"I could work for him . . . I could scrub and slave . . . on my knees!" she declared.

"I wonder if it would make him happy to have you grow callouses on those very pretty knees?" he asked. "Isn't the real question what Kildare wants to become?"

She was silent for a moment. Then she said: "Why couldn't he be both things? Why couldn't he belong to you and the hospital, and to me?"

Gillespie said: "Because I want his heart's blood for his work; and you want Paris hats."

"I don't want them. I hate them!" cried Rosalie. "I could wear sackcloth."

"He's seen you as pretty and gay as a humming-bird; would he be happy if you turned into a drab little sparrow, for his sake?"

"I've said all I can say," she answered, rising. "I think I'd better be going, doctor, if you don't mind."

"Please sit down," said Gillespie. "Let's work out a little more clearly the sort of a future he would have with you."

She exclaimed, desperately: "Everybody in the whole district knows him and loves him. If he hung out a shingle he'd have all the practice. He'd make thirty thousand a year!"

"That's more than an honest doctor needs," answered Gillespie. "And as a matter of fact, money is not what Kildare wants, is it? What *does* he want, Rosalie, outside of you?"

"I *could* make him happy," she cried.

"I think you could, in a way. I think you could make any man happy, in a way," he told her. "But what does Kildare have in his heart to be?"

His question forced the words slowly from her. "He wants to be like you," she admitted. Then, her voice choking, she added: "Are you going to take him away from me?"

She was astonished to hear him answer: "I couldn't."

She stared at him, comprehension coming slowly. He added: "You're stronger with Kildare than the whole rest of the world, including me. Nothing that anyone can do will take him from you."

"I see," whispered Rosalie. "You want me to send him away?"

She closed her eyes, tasting the pain of that thought inwardly and deeply, and in this moment of interval, Gillespie leaned a little forward with a gleam of triumph that made his face savage. He had settled back in his chair before she roused herself again.

"I won't do what you want. I won't do it!" she declared, trembling. "Why do you keep on talking?"

"Because you keep on listening," said Gillespie, "and the more you listen, the more I realise that you love Kildare. I'm begging for him but also I'm begging for myself."

"You? For *your*self?"

"I've eight or nine months left," said Gillespie, "and in that time I want to give the world what I've learned. Kildare's is the only brain I've found who can take what I know—and me. He's not able to take it now, but a little later he may be able to carry on. Will you leave him with me, Rosalie?"

She said, after a moment: "It's not true. You're trying to break me down. I know it's not true."

She went towards the door, hastily, and caught at the knob of it. Gillespie lowered his head and covered his face with his hands. So he offered her that melodramatic picture of despair and waited for it to take effect. Squinting through his fingers, he saw that the girl was hard-struck. Over her shoulder her frightened eyes stared back at him while she was pulling at the door vainly, as though it were locked.

"I'm not going to listen," she said.

Gillespie said, with his face still covered: "I have cancer. My body is riddled with malignant tumours. I hardly can live out eight months. But I might as well die tomorrow if there's no one who can be heir to all the gold I've piled up in my life. It's not the kind of gold that will buy Paris hats, though; and when I've given it to Kildare, it will not make him a penny richer in the pocket."

"I won't listen to you. It's not true." Rosalie stood back against the door, still warding off his words with a raised hand. Then she began to weep.

She said, whispering: "You're going to take him away from me. You're going to take him away!"

"I can't take him," said Gillespie. "You'd have to give him, Rosalie. That's the only way."

She sank into a chair in the corner. Gillespie picked up a telephone and murmured into it: "Now, please."

He added, aloud: "I've asked someone to come and take care of you. I've given up trying to fight you, Rosalie, and I'm sorry that I've hurt you so much."

She was moaning: "I'll never give him up! I'll never, never give him up!"

A nurse came in, a vague figure in the blinded eyes of Rosalie. Gillespie was saying, "Miss Lamont, this lady has just had rather a bad shock. Will you take her in the next room and do something for her?"

Rosalie got up and went across the room in an unhappy trance, with Mary Lamont guiding her. At the door, she ventured one glance through her tears towards Gillespie, but he seemed totally oblivious of her, sitting with his old face once more buried in his hand. It was not until she had left that he raised his head and smiled, a twisting grin that worked his mouth awry.

Rosalie lay back in a chair in the next room while Mary Lamont put the fold of a wet towel across her eyes.

"I'm not crying any more. I'm all right. I don't want you bothering," said Rosalie.

"It's no bother," said Mary Lamont.

She brought a freshly chilled towel, carefully wrung out and folded again. With this she replaced the first one and pressed it gently down over the eyes of Rosalie.

"I should have known!" murmured Rosalie. "I should have guessed that he'd be too much for me. Why—why—why did I ever come near him!"

She bit her lips and rallied, sitting up and removing the towel.

"I'll be all right now," she said. "Is there a mirror?"

Mary Lamont showed her to a mirror and stood by at a discreet distance as Rosalie touched up her make-up, with a stretching grimace of the mouth to give a firm surface when she applied the lipstick. When the colour was in place, Rosalie gave the mirror a smile.

She was reshaping her hair a little with her fingers when she turned from the mirror and asked, "Will I do now?"

"Of course—perfectly," said Mary.

Rosalie looked at her for the first time with observant eyes. Then she remembered, and was shocked. "You're Jimmy Kildare's nurse!" she exclaimed.

"I work in the dispensary with Doctor Kildare," Mary corrected.

Rosalie hardly heard the answer. The words she was reading so much more eagerly were all written in the face of the other girl.

"How did it happen—how do you come to be here?" she demanded.

"Doctor Gillespie called for me," said Mary.

"Just for you—specially?" said Rosalie. "Ah, I guess I understand."

She went towards the door, watching Mary Lamont askance.

"Shall I show you out?" asked the nurse.

"Show me *out*? . . . I guess you've shown me enough already," said Rosalie. "You're the object lesson, aren't you? But I'll be able to find the rest of the way."

She jerked the door open and turned to throw a few barbed words at the other girl, but the steady, un-aggressive eyes of Mary changed her mind. Rosalie merely said, "Well—so long—and thanks —" and as she went out she defied the nurse and all that she stood for with a flash of that smile which she assumed for street-wear because it would last so long.

XIX

BULL IN A BULLET SHOP

Happy Leeman had a head start towards a jovial existence because he had been gifted with a body so exceptional that it could absorb all the physical buffets of the world and laugh at them. He stood a couple of inches under six feet but he was fat with muscle which had grown without effort on his part. His girth was as hard as a barrel. And if he worked as a stevedore from time to time it was because the ponderous burdens which cracked the tendons of larger men were mere toys to the cushioned power of Happy.

He had not very much length of neck, and when he talked he had a way of lowering his chin against his chest and smiling, so that he seemed to be apologising for what he said, and making sly fun of himself.

Kildare, entering his room, found Happy spilled on a couch bed with his hands folded behind his head. The wall was decorated with pictures of racehorses, clipped from Sunday supplements. Happy did not rise, but extended a friendly hand and said, "Hi, it's the doc himself. How are you, doc? I hear you been having bad luck, eh?"

"Not as bad for me as for Nick," said Kildare, taking a

chair. "That's why I'm here. He asked me to come over and see you."

"Yeah? Did he?" asked Happy.

"He seems to think you're about his best friend," said Kildare, "and it might be that you could cheer him up if you made a call on him."

"I can do that and I will," stated Happy. "Have a shot?"

"No, thanks."

Happy, without sitting up, reached a bottle from the niche behind his bed, picked up a glass from the same shelf, and tipped out three wide fingers of rye. He balanced this for a time above his face, and then, opening his mouth wide, he poured in the drink, keeping the glass at a distance, and letting only a small stream fall.

"I used to drink from the bottle, but sometimes you get careless, doing that," said Happy, lighting a cigarette.

His apelike agility and control made him perfectly at home even when he was lying flat on his back. Instead of turning his head, he possessed an almost birdlike ability to roll his eyes, and in this manner he gave his attention to Kildare.

"How's the kid, anyway?" asked Happy.

"He's worried about dying," said Kildare. "He knows what comes after a murder; and he's worried about the electric chair."

"Is he?" asked Happy, smiling at the ceiling. "Well, it's rotten luck he's had. He shouldn't of shot so straight."

"He swears he didn't do it," said Kildare.

"Swearing won't save him."

"No," said Kildare, "he'll have to depend on the police."

"On the police? They're the boys that'll strap him into the chair, ain't they?"

"Between you and me," said Kildare, "they have a theory that Nick had nothing to do with the killing of Smith."

"Have they? Yeah, they always got theories," said Happy. "That's why they're always so kind of funny. Theories don't send guys to the chair."

"This one will, they think," answered Kildare.

"The hell you say!" murmured Happy, blowing his smoke out so strongly that it flattened out right against the ceiling in a blue-brown ring of curling mist.

"But Nick isn't quite sure he's safe, and he needs his friends to get the bad pictures out of his mind. He's seen a picture of the smoke rising out of the body in the chair . . ."

Happy shuddered and cursed under his breath.

"It always does, you know," said Kildare. "The first shock merely knocks out the man in the chair. The second pull of the switch sends through the current that burns him. And that's what kills."

"Like—like frying a chicken—greasy kitchen smoke!" said Happy.

"Yes. Like frying a chicken alive," said Kildare.

Happy reached for the bottle again and took a good swallow down his throat. The strength of the liquor made his face shine with sweat.

"It makes the kid nervous, does it?" said Happy.

"So you'd better see him and try to cheer him up. He thinks that you're a great fellow."

"Yeah—you know the way kids are," said Happy.

"But, of course, there's no real danger ahead of him," said Kildare. "The police have worked out their idea pretty thoroughly."

"Have they? What sort of an idea is it?"

"I don't think I should tell you, should I? But you'll keep it to yourself, won't you?"

"Tight as a stone," agreed Happy, and rolled his eyes suddenly sideways until they reached sight of Kildare and froze on their mark.

"They only have to find somebody who had a grudge against Smith and was a friend of Nick."

"Everybody had a grudge against Smith," said Happy, chuckling.

"But not everybody was a friend of Nick. The idea," said Kildare, going on glibly, "is that the man with the grudge against Smith first must have told Nick that Smith was talking about Rosalie. You see? That would make Nick angry enough to threaten Smith. When everybody knew that there was bad blood between them, this person watched for his chance. He saw Nick step out on the sidewalk after Smith, and he followed. He intended to drop the pair of them and have it look like a fatal gun fight. So he shot Smith first and then Nick; but Nick managed to live and to crawl away."

"It's too complicated," said Happy, staring at the ceiling again. "Complicated gadgets like that never mean nothing in court."

"I'm not so sure of that," answered Kildare. He leaned forward. "They think they know a man who was a friend of Smith and a friend of Nick. They think they'll fit him into the chair, before the switch is pulled on Nick. It won't be Nick who tries to jump—after he's dead."

"It won't be Nick?" repeated Happy Leeman.

He kept his eyes frozen on Kildare, reaching with his left hand for the whisky bottle at the same instant. But in the midst of this gesture Happy changed his mind.

He swung himself off the bed and grasped Kildare by the loose folds of coat, necktie, and shirt. His ribs, like heaving bellows, forced out a thundering voice. The gibbering of the lips gave the words only a dim enunciation as he shouted:

"What kind of a finger are you trying to put on me? If I bust you wide open, what kind of ideas am I gonna find inside of you?"

He crashed Kildare back against the wall as he spoke. But something else happened from behind and above Kildare, then. He saw the shadow and heard the fall of a blow, and Happy slid out on the floor on his face, with a long stroke of red paint drawn at the parting of his hair.

"What's the big idea, brother?" asked Weyman's voice. "Trying to have all the fun yourself?"

Kildare had no breath to answer, for the moment. He went to the chest of drawers and started by opening the bottom one. There was no need to go farther. The automatic was not even covered by the clothes inside. He stood up with the gun in his hand.

"The police have the bullet from the body of Smith,"

said Kildare, "and I think their ballistics people will find that it came from this gun—along with this slug that I took from Nick's chest. You get the three exhibits to 'em, will you? . . . And thanks, Weyman."

"Thanks for what?" asked Weyman. "But why don't you give me free tickets to your parties, doc? Why do I have to crash the gate?"

XX

CLINICAL NOTE

Afterwards, when the police had Happy Leeman with a harder grip than even his hands could break, Kildare got to a telephone and rang Rosalie, but she was not home. So he headed for the hospital and the surgical ward to tell Nick.

The news was all over the place before him. When he got in through the front door of the place a lurking figure with a camera appeared in the hall from the waiting-room and said: "Doctor James Kildare? Pardon me, doctor, but . . ."

"It's all right," said Kildare, and pushed his hand in the camera's face as the flash went off. He hurried down the hall with the reporter cursing behind him.

The elevator boy said: "Nice work, doc. Happy Leeman . . . Gee!"

Kildare said: "That's nonsense. Big Weyman was the fellow who handled . . ."

"Yeah, that mug; yeah, I know," said the elevator boy, preferring to stick to the story as he first had heard it.

But that did not matter. What was important was to see that the news had reached Nick, and then that Rosalie heard it. Down the corridor towards the surgical ward, he passed a pair of nurses prematurely old, as weary nurses are apt to look. He felt them turning to look after him. And when elderly nurses look after a young physician it means a very definite kind of name and fame.

Kildare went through the doorway. Nick saw him, and shouted and waved. The policeman got up and offered his place. Rosalie stood up, too.

She began to laugh, when she saw Kildare. She shook hands with him, still laughing.

"Look at him, Nick," she said. "Doesn't he look like a nice little preacher or something, the way he blushes? He saved you, Nick, but I almost thought he'd have to save me before he got around to you. Don't take it too big . . he was going to *marry* me!"

The policeman had heard part of this. He did not understand and backed away from hearing any of the rest. But Kildare understood, well enough, or thought he did. Somehow he waited for Nick to say something, but Nick lay looking at the ceiling with his face screwed into a hard knot.

"Oh, Jimmy," said Rosalie, "you're not going to be sour about it, are you? Maybe I *will* marry you some day, if you're good."

Kildare turned and got away towards the entrance of the ward.

Behind him, Nick said, softly: "Hold everything, Rosalie. You did fine. Only you kind of laid it on. But you did fine. Hold everything and don't let yourself break down, now."

"No, I won't break down," said Rosalie. She lowered herself gradually to the edge of the bed again.

Nick twisted a little and stared at her keenly; his face was tight with the strain of a man who is walking close to danger.

"You had to do it," said Nick. "You had to cut him clean out of your life. You know that. It had to be an operation, and operations hurt."

"Shut up, will you?" whispered Rosalie.

"Hold on to something," said Nick. "Don't go and break down and spoil everything!"

"I won't spoil anything. . . . Is he gone?" said Rosalie.

"Yeah. He's gone out of the door, now. Rosalie, can you smile?"

"Oh, God," said Rosalie, "I wish . . . I wish . . ."

"You wouldn't wish to grab the doc," stated Nick, scowling. "You wouldn't be that much rat. Smile, will you?"

"I'll try," said Rosalie.

"That's fine," said Nick. "That's swell . . ."

"Did—did Gillespie see me throw him out?" she asked.

"He saw it all from his wheelchair," said Nick. "I watched him take it."

"I hope he burns," whispered Rosalie. "I hope he burns good. Did he laugh?"

"He didn't laugh a lick. Rosalie, keep on smiling, will you?"

Kildare got somehow through the door. He saw Gillespie, then, backing his wheelchair to cut him off and waving a hand at Carew, for the head of the hospital was

187

coming down the corridor in a happy humour. Carew waved and began to talk loudly, from a distance.

Carew said: "You shouldn't have been so tongue-tied with me, Kildare. That was a very efficient piece of detective work you did by teaming with that man Flaherty. I suppose you know that Flaherty has made a fine statement giving most of the credit to you? An excellent piece of work, Kildare."

"Kildare," Gillespie snapped, "why haven't I that report from you on the lobar pneumonia slides I sent you?"

"As a matter of fact, sir," said Kildare, "for several days I haven't seen the slides and —"

"Several days?" cried Gillespie. "Several damnations! Can't I get men to carry on for me unless I keep my eye on them night and day? Go back to that office and get at those slides now, young man."

"Back—to my old office?" said Kildare, incredulously.

"Isn't that where the slides are?" said Gillespie. "We've been losing time. We've been losing thousands of time."

He stopped and for an instant he stared at the silent Kildare. Then he made an abrupt, impatient gesture with his hand. "Well?" he snapped.

"Thank you, sir," said Kildare.

"Now there's a funny fellow," said Gillespie. "He thanks me for damning him with a hard job. Where's the girl with the sallow look? Lamont, help him to get his stuff in order. The man surrounds himself with the most damnable confusion in the world. And—Kildare!"

"Yes, sir?" answered Kildare.

He stood before the wheelchair, looking into Gillespie's

face and trying to keep out of his own face any evidence of the despair and the exultation that were struggling inside of him.

"While she's helping you, you might find out why that girl has thrown away about ten years of her life in the last ten days."

Kildare looked at the nurse with the whole weary pain of existence in his eyes.

He turned to Gillespie.

"I'll attempt a diagnosis, sir," he said, and went slowly on down the hall with Mary Lamont a proper half step behind him.

THE END